W9-BIF-176

A STONE OF THE HEART

A STONE OF THE HEART

TOM GRIMES

FOUR WALLS EIGHT WINDOWS
NEW YORK

Published by:
Four Walls Eight Windows
PO Box 548
Village Station
New York, N.Y. 10014

First edition.
First printing April 1990.

Library of Congress Cataloging-in-Publication Data
Grimes, Tom, 1954–
A stone of the heart/by Tom Grimes.—1st ed.
p. cm.
ISBN: 0-941423-40-9
I. Title.
PS3557.R489985S7 1990
813′.54—dc20 89-49724
CIP

Cover and text designed by Cindy LaBreacht.

Printed in the U.S.A.

Too long a sacrifice
Can make a stone of the heart . . .

W. B. YEATS

FOR JODY

AND FOR MY FAMILY

CHAPTER ONE

The day my father was arrested, Roger Maris hit his sixty-first home run. At the time, I was fourteen. My father had just come home from work. He was wearing what he wore to the office every day—a shabby raincoat, a fedora, and a suit so shiny with wear that I could nearly see my reflection in it. Under his arm he carried the afternoon edition of the *Journal American.* The sports pages were tracking the final at-bats of Roger Maris's assault on Babe Ruth's single season home run record. I picked up the paper after he had laid it down and began memorizing the day's box score. The thought of Babe Ruth's record being surpassed loomed majestically in my imagination at the time. The feat seemed so herculean compared to the accomplishments and work of my father.

I had stopped saying hello to him when he came home because he dismissed it as an annoyance. We had entered into a guarded, largely inarticulate relationship shortly after I reached my teens, and now any civility we showed one another was merely a matter of habit.

"Where's your mother?" he said to me as he was hanging his coat.

"In the kitchen."

He walked by Rudy, my younger brother, who was lying on the floor coloring. He kicked the sole of Rudy's shoe. "Don't you say hello?" he asked.

Rudy looked up at him over his shoulder, but said nothing. This wasn't unusual. Rudy never spoke to anyone. Six years old and he hadn't said a word. He spent all his time coloring, drawing pictures of monsters locked in cages, shackled by chains. My parents had taken him to several doctors, each of whom said that there was no indication of a physical deformity that would impair Rudy's ability to speak. It seemed that Rudy simply preferred not to. None of us was entirely sure why and, as Rudy wasn't telling, we ignored him to a large extent, treating his silence as if it were a minor annoyance or childhood affliction like the measles. Rudy looked away from my father and went back to coloring, and my father walked into the kitchen.

My mother was sitting there, reading a paperback novel, a romance lifted from the supermarket rack while waiting to check out groceries. Fame and wealth, or wealth and sex—the mass market ying-yang, escapism at popular prices. It was the stuff of soap operas and melodramatic movies and my mother ate it up. In fact, she seemed not to read the novels as fiction, but rather as oracular how-to. She was a dreamer. In a way, she condescended to her peers, the women in the neighborhood who went out in housecoats and curlers, frayed winter coats and scuffed slippers. She believed that our lower-class status was temporary. My grandfather had been a successful coat manufacturer. He'd made a lot of money and my mother had been brought up with a sense of security and expectation. She overlooked the fact, however, that my grandfather lost the money once he'd made it, investing unwisely and with a naïve but authoritarian heedlessness. When she did acknowledge our situation, she covered it over by believing that, with her help, my father would climb the corporate ladder to success. News of this came late, and evidently as a surprise to my father. He was a clerk—though my mother insisted he was a junior executive—in a freight forwarding office, a nine to fiver with a less promising future than Bob Cratchett's. Making something of himself, he would later tell me, was not something he had even considered when he married my mother. Planning, he said, was not his strong point. Perhaps what he meant was that he didn't understand that he could be made to feel worthless if he didn't. This may or may not be true, and remains, as it will continue to remain, unasked. All that is certain is the fact that he drank himself beyond both the point at which he was still able to retain control of his own life, and the point at which he cared whether or not he did.

"What are we eating?" he said to my mother. I looked over the back of the armchair and could see him standing in the kitchen doorway, my mother seated at the table in front of him. She put her book down and looked at him.

"Chicken," she said.

"Is it almost ready? I have to go out."

My mother was startled by this news, though she tried to mask it. My father had been dry—that is, off the sauce—for six weeks. He had been toeing the line, going to work every day, staying in every night. To my mother, any change in this pattern meant trouble. "Where?" she asked.

"Out."

"We have my niece's wedding to go to this weekend."

"So what?"

"I don't want anything to go wrong."

"What's that mean?"

"Nothing."

"Yeah, right." He unbuttoned his shirt sleeves.

"Where are you going?"

"Pantano's wife died, I'm going to the wake. You got any more fucking questions, or is the interrogation over?"

"I'm not interrogating you. And don't talk that way when the kids can hear you."

We had heard it before. I had, at least. The day Rudy was born my father and I went to see him in the hospital. A hefty nurse escorted us into the nursery and pointed Rudy out to us. He was lying in a crib behind a glass enclosure, nondescript, silent, asleep. The nurse left and my father and I stood there, staring at Rudy. My father had his hands on his hips and seemed to be displeased. He took a cigarette out of his shirt pocket, lit it, then stared at Rudy a few moments longer. He turned his head, looked down at the floor, his upper front teeth biting into his lower lip as he said, "Fuck."

"When did his wife die?" my mother asked him.

"Yesterday."

"Well why didn't you say something then?"

"Because I didn't know till today, OK!"

"All right, all right."

They paused, seeming to despise each other silently, like the faithful taking a moment to consider their sins.

"I'll send a Mass card," my mother said.

My father was removing his tie. "Don't do anything. I'm going to the wake, that's the end of it." He looked at her for a moment. "I'm going to change my clothes," he said.

"Well I'll go with you."

"No, you won't."

"What do you mean, I won't? How can you go without me?"

"By going. All right?"

My father turned and walked out of the kitchen. A

few minutes later, my mother called Rudy and me to the table for dinner. When my father returned he was wearing a dark blue Brooks Brothers suit. It had taken him nearly a year to pay off the installments on it, but to him, I suppose, it possessed a certain liberating elegance and power. He told my mother to mind her own business the day he brought it home and she asked how much it cost. It seemed he didn't want it tainted by considerations of money. He never wore the suit to work and the shirt he had on with it was a white, hand-tailored cotton one which he had had made for himself before marrying my mother. The knot of his tie was secured by a solid gold tie-bar stuck through the stays of the shirt's collar. My father was a handsome man—auburn hair, blue matinee-idol's eyes, perfect aquiline nose. Sleek as a stallion. But that evening there was a restlessness about him, an irritability and curtness which marked the timbre of his moods whenever he was feeling caged and depressed. There was something wild about him, as if he had been transformed into pure trouble.

"How are you getting to the wake?" my mother asked him.

"I'm taking the car. How do you think?" he said, referring to the battleship grey Chrysler sedan, a ten-year-old hand-me-down with bald tires and a dented fender that was given us by my grandfather.

"Are you sure you don't want me to go with you?"

"Positive."

My mother let the conversation breathe silently for a moment in order to emphasize the incidental thrust of her next remark.

"I had thought of going to the movies tonight," she said. "'A Place in the Sun' with Elizabeth Taylor and Montgomery Clift is back."

"So go," my father said.

"I didn't want to go by myself. I wanted to go together."

"So you bring it up now when you know I can't go. Every chance you get you turn the screw, don't you?"

"I was just making conversation."

"Don't be so sure."

"Why do you have to jump on everything I say? I made an innocent comment about going to see a movie."

"Yeah, right. You want to see the movie, see the movie. Do what you want."

Rudy had his sketch pad and pencils on the dinner table. He was drawing another one of his monster portraits. In this one, the monster had burst out of its chains and bent back the bars of its cell. In a speech balloon above its head, Rudy had written the word "Roar!" He hadn't eaten a morsel of food and I eyed his untouched dinner. If Rudy had to be coaxed into eating, I was just the opposite. At five foot six, I weighed one hundred and sixty pounds. One of the nuns had studied my annual height and weight card when I was in grammar school and said, "This won't do, Michael. This simply won't do." I wasn't sure what she meant. Was I too fat to learn? Was my brain about to atrophy, collapsing under the relentless burden of planning midnight snacks? As I rose into puberty, I became acutely aware of being overweight. Yet, I couldn't bring myself to care. Food was my sole pleasure. It was succoring and unjudging, and I buried myself and my insecurity deeply within it.

"Mom," I said.

My mother was still arguing with my father and didn't hear me.

"Mom," I said, louder this time. I waited for her to pay attention to me, but she didn't. "MOM!" I shouted.

"What?!"

"Rudy's not eating his dinner. Can I finish it?"

"No. He's got to learn to start eating. Rudy," she said, turning to him, "start eating your dinner."

Rudy continued drawing, tilting his head a bit further downward.

"Rudy, pick up your fork and start eating," my mother said, enunciating her words slowly and clearly, as if they were being etched in stone.

Rudy ignored her and continued with his work.

"He's not going to eat it," I said.

"Rudy. Eat your dinner. Do you hear me? Eat your dinner!"

My father, who had been eating silently, sprung up, reached out, grabbed Rudy's dinner plate, and flung it across the table at the spot that my plate occupied. I put one forearm across my chest to deflect it and it caromed off my wrist and fell to the floor.

"He wants to starve to death," my father said, "let him. He'll die of starvation, the other one of obesity."

He threw his napkin down, turned, and left the kitchen. Rudy, my mother, and I heard him open the door to the closet where we hung our coats. The bare wooden hangers clattered as he searched among them for his topcoat. Then we heard him walking through the living room. He unlocked the front door, the sound of its lock tripping carrying a dead and final note back through the rooms. Then the door slammed shut, and a wake of silence opened up throughout the house.

My mother looked as if she was trying not to cry. Rudy and I sat at the table, instinctively sensing that our apparent tranquility glossed over the brutishness of what had happened. My mother stood up, went to the sink, and picked up a sponge. She rinsed it, then knelt down and began cleaning Rudy's dinner up off the floor.

"Call your grandmother," she told me as she scrubbed the stained spots. "Tell her to come over and watch Rudy. We're going to the movies."

CHAPTER TWO

My grandmother arrived while my mother was in her bedroom. When she came down she was carrying a sealed envelope addressed to Mr. Charles Pantano. As she was putting her coat on she told my grandmother which pajamas Rudy was to wear and what time he was to be in bed. There were a few terse, accusing words exchanged between my mother and grandmother, and then we left, my mother dismissing the argument as being none of my grandmother's business.

We walked along the dark, quiet streets to a mailbox, and when we reached one my mother pulled down the handle and dropped the envelope into the slot.

"It's a good thing for your father that I take care of things like this," she said. "He would never think of sending a Mass card. People notice these things, especially when you overlook them. Then they have something negative to say. If you want to be something, remember that."

In her plans for attaining a respectable position in the world, my mother did not overlook my potential. My grades were good and an unwitting teacher was naïve enough to release information about my IQ to my mother. I was bright, not brilliant. A slightly above average schoolkid. Nothing to get excited about. But to my mother, who clung to anything which raised her sense of self-esteem, it was a sign from God. She was among the chosen and I would help deliver her back into the bliss of fortune and respectability. I was destined, in my mother's mind, to become a figure in the history of Western culture whose achievements would dwarf the combined efforts of Einstein, F.D.R., and Jonas Salk. But her efforts to nurture my dependence on her failed. I was at least as willful as she was, and had no intention of giving in to her demands. We found ourselves involved in a leapfrogging progression in which one expected something of the other, and the other always failed to produce it. We grew into the roles of inferior substitutes, existing for one another in the shadow of an imaginary ideal, the urgency of our need, at times, driving us completely apart.

We turned onto Jamaica Avenue, the commercial street of the neighborhood, and walked along under the lights. It was quiet now, the traffic and shoppers having left for the night. The sidewalk and the blank faces of the three story buildings had turned from ash to black in the darkness, and only the bars were open, their neon signs flashing like warning lights on a deserted, unfamiliar road. As we passed them, one after the other, the silence which enveloped the street was cleaved by the din issuing from the open barroom doorways. I peered in through any number of them and saw through the smoky chiaroscuro the battered and vacant-looking faces of the drinkers, their hoarse shouting and coughing the only noise echoing along the street. During the afternoon, there was pandemonium on the street. Swarms of people and deafening noise—husbands screaming at their wives, mothers herding their broods back to rat-infested railroad flats above the street for dinner, the kids wailing, tears cutting streaks of light along their dirt-covered faces. Growling busses, honking car horns, and roaring trains could not drown out the screeching drunks who spilled out of the bars in fights, tearing at each other's hair, blood and dirt and sawdust coagulating in a thick, knotty clump on their scalps as the arid cold dried it. Everywhere it was chaos. The chaos bred violence, and out of the violence came destruction, and, with that, a kind of defeated order.

The only ones who seemed oblivious to the convulsion of collective despair were the local crazies. There was Jimmy Lyons, the forty-two year old failed stock room clerk. He dressed in a Brooklyn Dodgers uniform and played baseball with the grammar school kids in the park, if they let him. Derby wore a Bowie knife taped to the side of his highly polished G.I. boot, and seemed to have only two occupations—walking his dog, "Cunts," and shouting obscenities at the taxpayers. Even though he had never been in the service, he had a passion for fatigues and flak jackets. He lived with his mother at the end of a dead-end road near the church, and rarely left his bedroom, it seemed. Whenever a group of us walked by we could hear music coming from his window. Indecipherable, squealing. It turned out that Derby liked to listen to his records, which were supposed to be played at thirty-three and a half rpms, at seventy-eight. "Why?" one of us asked him once. "Cause then they sound like fucking mice." Fine, I thought. *You* argue with a guy carrying a knife as long as your forearm. And there was Randy. Every morning Randy appeared on the corner of Jamaica Avenue and Woodhaven Boulevard. Carrying a battered briefcase, he took up a post on one side of the street or the other—it didn't matter—and put his thumb out. When the light changed, he crossed the street, put down his briefcase, and stuck out his thumb, hitching in the other direction. He did this every morning of the week, except Sunday when he went to church. No one ever picked him up. No one ever asked him where he was going. He didn't have a job, but he liked to think he did in order to maintain a schedule of punctual and methodical madness. A functioning lunatic, limited and harmless, Randy fit in and, in time, became something of a landmark.

As we walked, my mother continued to talk about the importance of making a success of myself, while I attuned my senses to the rabid undertones of violence which echoed along the street. At night, it was roamed by neighborhood kids who, a year after graduating from grammar school, had metamorphosed from the meek to the malicious. Insecure, largely illiterate, they moved together in packs, their identities linked to the identity of the gang, the mass. With my mother I was fairly safe. They preyed only on other youths in the area, the fighting limited to intramural skirmishes among a network of playgrounds. Embryonic, their rage was restricted to their peers; it was not yet directed toward parents and society. The street was wet from an evening shower and the gang members huddled in shop doorways, the neon bar signs casting amethyst halos around their faces as they stood, sipping their beer, and watched us pass by.

As we rounded a bend in the street, the marquee of the movie house appeared, its luminous white panels hovering above the sidewalk. My anxiety subsided as the security and promise of the light enveloped us.

As we sat in the balcony's smoking section, waiting for the movie to begin, my mother tried to impress upon me the importance of cultivating connections with people in positions of power. "It's not what you know, it's who you know," she said, speaking as if from experience.

"Then I don't have to go to school," I said. "I could just meet people."

"Don't get smart," she said, and continued to mentally lay out the groundwork of my future. At the upcoming wedding I would again meet all of her successful relatives, men who ran factories and insurance offices, their private phobias and failings masked by large cars and terribly decorated houses.

"And this is Uncle Gus," she would say. "You remember Uncle Gus. He makes all those nice little fish-shaped plates. And those other things—what do you call them, Gus?"

"Trivets."

"Trivets, that's right." Score one for Uncle Gus.

Whenever we walked away from him, my mother would say, "He's a millionaire. He owns his own boat."

That was fine for Uncle Gus, I thought. But what did it have to do with me? Uncle Gus looked like a walrus. He constantly chewed the end of a long cigar, and whenever I shook his hand it felt like the sole of an old shoe, rough and gritty as sand. His wife, Rose, always wore the same dark brown evening gown to every wedding. She seemed to me as remote and unknowable as a mannequin. Not that she was pretty. The whiskers she'd forgotten to shave or bleach darkened her upper lip and, as she was heavy but insisted on wearing snug clothing, she had the blubbery homeliness of a seal.

I imagined myself standing in a group of uncles, quasi-uncles, and outright fake-uncles—my mother's penchant for allowing everyone even remotely connected with her family to assume the status of relative, coloring the limits of our extended family with a false sanctity. Each of the men would be wearing a blue, three-piece suit, the chains of their pocket watches stretched taut across their huge stomachs. "They all came from nothing," my mother would tell me, as she had a thousand times, "and now they all drive Cadillacs."

"Still gonna be the doctor there, kid?" Tony Bollo, a relative of dubious standing, asked me every time I saw him.

"I guess so."

"I guess so? What do you mean, you guess so? You're going to medical school. Ain't that right, Marie?" My mother nodded in agreement. "You be a doctor and make your mother proud," he said. Then, true to his low-level Mafia connections and streetwise beginnings, he leaned close to me and, pausing for comic effect, whispered, "Otherwise, I'll break your legs."

"Of course he's going to be a doctor," my mother said. "He has the highest IQ in his school. A teacher told me the other day."

Later, ensconced in a seat in the theatre's balcony, gorging myself on a third barrel of popcorn, I stopped imagining what would take place at the wedding long enough to be hypnotized by the scene in which Montgomery Clift tries to drown Shelley Winters. I was transfixed, as if I were studying a blueprint of my destiny. In my mind my mother had been magically transformed into the pathetic harridan on the screen. Her constant nagging at me to become a success—motivated by her own need for it—and her incessant prodding and cajoling, had me combing my memory for the locations of secluded lakes in our area. I didn't understand that the scene was more appropriate to my father's situation, just as I didn't understand that—in the rapture of her own fantasy—my mother identified herself with Elizabeth Taylor, the ravishing and untainted rich girl.

The movie was long and when we got home it was past ten o'clock. My father had not yet come home. My grandmother was sitting on the sofa, doing needlepoint. This was her hobby. Knitting sweaters, socks, gloves and scarves for her two beloved grandchildren occupied the other fifteen hours of her day. In every room we had a framed needlepoint. Cloyingly sentimental images of children with dogs, dogs with hunters. Scenes of Rockwellian innocence, holiday gatherings in worlds where children appeared well-adjusted, and the adults looked happy, healthy, and sober. I had hoped that my grandmother would have retired her hobby, thrown away her bifocals and taken to the streets with a tin cup and dark glasses. But she persisted, turning out new work at a pace which would have tired Picasso. My mother hung each one without regard to overkill, displaying every piece and saying to me, "Do you know how much these will be worth someday?" To whom, I wondered, even as I recalled this years later and, with the forgiving ardor brought on by distance, realized that my mother had always traded her own life for the profits of some vague and ill-imagined dream.

I went into the kitchen to prepare myself a bedtime snack, while my mother waited for my grandmother to leave. Opening the refrigerator door, I stood before a cornucopia of junk food—jello, imitation cheese, glutinous party dips—and tried to decide what to eat. While thinking it over, I ate a bowlful of cold, leftover macaroni. I knelt down, opened the cold cut bin, and studied its contents. I ate several slices of bologna and American cheese which I had rolled together into a tube and dipped into a jarful of mustard held between my thighs.

"What are you doing in there?" my mother shouted from the living room, where she was still bickering with my grandmother.

After swallowing, I said, "Nothing."

"I let you have three things of popcorn at the movies. I don't want you eating anymore. The doctor said you had to lose weight."

Yes, but we hadn't gotten a second opinion yet, I thought. "I'm not eating. I'm reading the paper."

"I can hear the refrigerator."

I screwed the top back onto the mustard jar, placed it on one of the door shelves, dropped the cold cuts into the bin, and closed the drawer. I continued looking over the pickings, peeking under aluminum foil which was tightly wrapped around plates and bowls, at the same time listening for footsteps. There was nothing in the refrigerator that really piqued my interest. I ate two cold pork chops, though my heart wasn't in it. I felt a strong craving for dessert, something sweet to cut the inert and greasy taste that the meat left on my tongue. There were donuts in the bread bin. That they had the texture of styrofoam since they were made by the million with the cheapest ingredients didn't matter to me. They were chocolate-covered and, perhaps even more important, familiar. There was a certain comfort and nostalgia in their synthetic sameness.

I stood up, walked to the cabinet in which we kept glasses, took one out, brought it to the refrigerator, and filled it with milk. I tugged the shirt tails out of my trousers and let them hang over my pants, down past my hips. I went to the bread bin, removed three donuts from the cardboard box they came in, closed it, and wrapped the donuts in a napkin.

"What are you still doing in there?" my mother said.

"Can I please finish reading this in peace, please?" I shouted back, really annoyed now.

I took several deep breaths, then sucked in my stomach and slipped the donuts inside the waistband of my pants. Gingerly, I grabbed the glass of milk and walked into the living room.

"I'm going to bed," I said, trying not to expend too much oxygen on words.

"What are you doing with a glass of milk?"

"It helps me sleep." I started up the stairs, climbing daintily so as not to crush my stash.

"Don't you kiss us goodnight?" my grandmother said.

"I have to go to the bathroom," I said. Three quarters of the way up the stairs they were no longer in sight. When I reached the top step I heard my mother say, "Goodnight." Safe, I removed the donuts from my trousers, went into my room, and locked the door.

Rudy was in his bed asleep and I could hear his faint snoring. I switched on the lowest of the three light bulbs attached to a lamp pole extending from floor to ceiling beside my bed. I turned the casing which covered the bulb so the light shined directly on Rudy's face, managing to annoy him now, tired as I was, purely by instinct. I undressed, and while I was naked I caught a glimpse of myself in the mirror which hung above my bureau. I was enormous. There were two thick crescents of fat hanging from my pectorals and my navel was deep and wide enough to hold a walnut. Over my hips were bands of flesh as thick and soft as a loaf of packaged bread. Beneath my stomach the wild, unfinished hairs growing above my genitals seemed pathetic. After covering myself with my pajamas, I climbed into bed. I was depressed to the point that I didn't want to eat the donuts, but past the point at which I possessed the resolve not to. To distract myself, I turned on the television, an ancient black and white set we had inherited from a friend of my father's. I watched Groucho Marx torment the contestants on "You Bet Your Life," then a rerun of "The Honeymooners." When I finished eating, I shut the set off and turned the light away from

Rudy, checking to see if he was still sleeping. He was. I slid out of bed and went over to the desk where I did my homework. I opened the bottom drawer and shuffled through a morass of school papers. Midway through the pile was the book I had found in my mother's dresser drawer. It was called CANDY and the jacket claimed that it was sensationally erotic. I had discovered it one day while I was poking around in my parents' room. I hadn't been looking for anything in particular, I just wondered what kind of life they kept secret from Rudy and me. I didn't give much thought to whether or not my mother would notice that it was missing. It seemed unlikely, as it was buried beneath clothes she no longer wore—leopard skin-patterned stretch pants and midriff blouses. I got back into bed and began rereading a scene toward the end of the book, one I had nearly committed to memory. In it, Candy is deflowered by Buddha in a crumbling temple. Nice mix of soft core porn and religious taboo. Two sentences into it I had a boner the size of a kosher pickle. I forgot about how much I weighed, about medical school and the presidency, about my parents' problems and bitterness, about Rudy's silence. I even forgot about Roger Maris. I had a date with Candy.

CHAPTER THREE

When I awoke, I found that my mother had been sitting up all night in the kitchen, crying. Although I knew the answer, I asked anyway. "What's wrong?" I said.

"Your father hasn't come home yet."

I was silent for a moment, then said, "Did he call?"

She shook her head. Her elbows were propped on the formica top of the table, her hands clasped together and pressed to her lips as if she was praying. I knew that she was worried, and had every reason to be. This was an all-too-familiar scene, an early morning spent wondering where my father was. It had the earmarks of one of his benders, unexplained disappearances and week-long drunks.

"Maybe he went straight to work," I suggested. Up until the preceding spring I had been totally helpless whenever this happened. But at fourteen I had begun to develop an independence which must have seemed reliable and supportive to my mother. "What should I do?" my mother suddenly asked me the last time, and with that simple appeal for advice I emerged, in a way, from the role of child and was asked to be an adult. I quickly found that I was more rational in these circumstances than my mother, perhaps because I had less to lose. My father would always be my father, there was no changing that. But my father did not always have to be my mother's husband. So when she asked me to help, I tried to.

"If he had gone into the office he would have called," she said. "I can't call asking for him if he's not there."

"I suppose not," I said. After that came mental paralysis. There was no simple solution to the problem; there was no remedy but waiting.

It was nearly eight o'clock. "You'd better get dressed for school," my mother said.

"What if he doesn't come home?"

"I'll call the school if anything happens."

"I'm not going to be able to concentrate in class, so what's the point?" School was a dull and dispiriting place to me, and once I saw an opportunity to miss a day of it, I was not above using my father's truancy as an excuse to.

"You've missed so much school already this year," my mother said.

"I'm doing fine," I said. "We're not learning anything anyway. It's freshman year. They're just trying to find out who we are." Mixing a partial truth with an outright lie, I hoped to create for my mother an image of such casualness on the part of the teachers that it would seem I had been vacationing for the entire first month of the semester.

She was silent for several moments. I knew that she was weighing my best interests, but also taking into consideration her own needs. It would be less lonely with me around and, possibly, somehow less desperate. Once I understood this, I felt cheap and manipulative.

"Can you call a friend to get your homework assignments?"

"Absolutely."

"Make sure."

"I will."

With that settled, my mother and I lost the momentum of conversation. Without the distraction of petty details, time seemed to slow and balloon. We were left with just waiting, and staring at each other across the table. My mother went back to worrying, I went back to thinking of ways to keep her from worrying, and, after a few minutes, realized that there were none.

"Do you want me to do anything?" I asked. My words made me feel stupid. What could I do? "I mean, like is there anything you want me to do?" I said, rebounding gracefully. I felt no less foolish, but at least somewhat earnest.

My mother looked at me and, after a moment, put out her arms and said, "Come here and give me a hug."

I didn't want to. I had reached an age—or a point in my life—at which I was no longer certain how I felt toward either my mother or my father. Loving them seemed natural, but the uncritical period of that love had passed. I no longer felt comfortable exchanging any sort of affection with either of them. After fourteen years, the conundrum of their relationship had by turns hurt and frustrated me time and again until finally I began to see—as if it had suddenly become opaque—the distance by which we were separated. Yet I could not bring myself to say no to my mother. Not because I lacked the meanness it would have required—though that was part of it—but because I was uncertain as to how ready I was to have that feeling of distance become permanent. As much as I wanted not to go to her, I did. She held her arms out and hugged me, her arms circling my shoulders as she sat in the chair, while I, standing between her legs, allowed her to silently rock us. I heard her begin to cry, quietly. That triggered in me the same need, the same indulgence and longing for release. It seemed natural to give in to it, a confirmation of our helplessness, an acceptance of it. But I saw it as a trap, something I didn't want to be caught in, and I stopped myself.

"It'll be OK," I said to her. I let my arms hang by my sides, not touching her, not hugging her back. We were silent for a few moments. "I should get Rudy up and make breakfast," I said. And as I pulled away from her, she opened her arms and let me go.

I walked into the living room and from the foot of the stairs yelled to Rudy to wake up. I went to the front door and picked up the morning paper, removing the rubber band which some other, more industrious, high school kid had fastened it with at five o'clock that morning. Unfolding the paper, I turned it over to the back page and began poring over the sports section. In my estimation, hard news was the pennant race. If a guy landed on the moon, or the two hemispheres were annihilated by thermonuclear devices, someone would tell me about it. Standing in the doorway, I read the coverage of the preceding day's Yankee game. Maris had hit his sixtieth. There were three games left in the season, at best a dozen chances to break Ruth's record. I was obsessive about the quest, following it all through our restless summer as if it had the power to restore order and a sense of hope to my family's life. Morning, afternoon, and evening sports sections of three city newspapers, the weekly *Sports Illustrated*, I read them all, memorized the statistics, compared Maris's pace with Ruth's. That Maris's record was already tainted by the one hundred and sixty-two game season—Ruth had hit sixty in one hundred and fifty-four games—only served to humanize him for me. After hitting his sixtieth, the press had descended on him. I imagined that he felt trapped, cornered, and made over into someone he didn't want to be. When I finished the article I went back into the house to prepare breakfast.

Rudy had not come downstairs yet. He was ordinarily up by seven o'clock, so I called him a second time, then walked into the kitchen where my mother was hanging up the phone. I put the paper down on the table and walked to the refrigerator.

"Your grandparents are coming over," my mother said.

"I heard."

"Can you take care of breakfast? I need to go lie down."

"No problem."

"Make Rudy's for him when he comes down."

"Uh-huh."

"Call me if you need me for anything, or if anybody calls."

"I will."

My mother stood there looking at me, as if she expected something, then finally turned and left the room.

I took a carton of frozen waffles from the freezer, opened it, and dropped two waffles into the toaster, pushing the lever down until it caught and the inside of the box began to glow. Outside in the yard some leaves were beginning to yellow on the trees, a dull flat color in the greyish light. A sweet, almost synthetic smell began to fill the room and brought my attention back inside the house. I opened one of the cabinets, took out a plate, set it on the table beside a knife and fork, and creased a paper napkin. The toaster ticked steadily. The first set of waffles popped up and I lifted them out and replaced them with two others, leaving the first two on top of the toaster to keep warm. We kept a huge bottle of cheap maple syrup in the pantry closet. My mother had hidden it behind cereal boxes and cans of vegetables and off-price soup. The second pair of waffles came up, knocking the first set to the counter top, while I was carrying the bottle to the table, and after setting it down I tossed the waffles onto the plate and set it on the table. I took out a glass and a bottle of Bosco, put them beside my plate, and sat down. I opened the paper to the daily baseball column, poured some syrup over the waffles, and put the first piece of tasteless dough into my mouth as I began to read.

One of the local columnists—a notoriously sentimental scribe given to fits of boilermaker-induced despair—made a case for Maris's feat, and by extension baseball itself, as being a way out of our national death wish. Nuclear annihilation, the Cold war. Appalachian poverty and inner city ghettoes. The game would lead us to the light. Right, I thought. Sure.

I read the other columns and articles on the upcoming game. Writers compared Maris's at-bat home run percentage with Ruth's, the old guard seeming to slight Maris's effort, as if his challenging of Ruth's record was somehow blasphemous. Ruth's record was a constant in a world that was naturally in a state of flux. There was a nostalgia and security attached to it, something firm and untainted which many were slow to relinquish. The fact that Maris had hit sixty home runs in six hundred and eighty-four at bats, Ruth in six hundred eighty-seven, was hardly mentioned. To question the unassailability of Ruth's record, to tamper with the established order, was somehow almost subversive.

Rudy came into the kitchen as I finished reading. He stood on the other side of the table looking at me. In one hand he had a drawing pad and some colored pencils. Unlike me, and unusual for him, Rudy had removed his pajamas and was wearing only his underwear. Rudy did not normally dress or undress himself. My mother had to do it for him. If she didn't, I imagine that he would simply have stayed in one outfit or another until the clothes rotted off him. So I wasn't sure if his appearance in underwear was an attempt and failure, or some sort of protest, a statement against the chaos of our life and daytime clothing in general.

"Rudy, what are you doing in your underwear?" I said.

He didn't answer. Instead, he stared at me with a look of impervious obliviousness, a concentrated effort at being a cipher.

"You want to tell me why I bother asking?" I said. He ignored me.

Rudy had a round head that was roughly the size of a large cantaloupe. He was fair, like our father, and his features seemed designed to make him inconspicuous. He had a small, plain nose; thin, flesh-colored lips; light brown eyes, and dun-colored hair which was clipped to within half an inch of his skull. His face seemed to deny recollection. I could never picture it in my mind. If he was not in front of me, my memory could not reconstruct his features. It was eerie, once I'd realized it. And I wondered if it might have been related to the fact that I had never heard him speak.

I began to ask Rudy if he wanted breakfast, then thought better of it and simply pointed to the chair opposite the one I was sitting in. Rudy laid his pad and pencils on the table, pulled the chair back, and sat down.

I made him some waffles, put them on a plate, poured syrup over them, and set the plate in front of him. Rudy drank nothing but water. Even when he was an infant he had to be force fed his formula. Amazingly thin, he occasionally reminded me of stem and flower, his thin body supporting a head too large for it. At six, Rudy was not much taller than a foot stool and weighed less than forty pounds. My mother tried forcing him to eat more, but he had greater endurance than she did, than any of us actually, and so we allowed him to hover around us in his undernourished, seemingly stunted state, and forgot about trying to correct it on our more selfish days. I set a glassful of water in front of him, then sat down to read the remainder of the paper.

"Are you finished?" I asked him when I was through reading. A piece of waffle the size of a movie theater ticket was all that was missing from his plate and he was gently scratching at the surface of his pad with the tip of one of his colored pencils. I waited, thinking—out of habit—that there might be an answer, then gave up when he simply looked up at me as if I were a thundercloud, something incomprehensible and noisy passing by overhead.

"Forget it," I said, and took the plate away from him.

I cleared my dish and washed them both before my grandmother arrived. When she did, the cleaning and straightening and complaining would begin. She would have her say about my father's disappearance. Why, I wondered, did my mother call her parents when we were having trouble? A common reaction in most families, I imagined; in ours it was an act of sheer stupidity. There was something masochistic in it as well, even though it was reassuringly cyclical, like my father's benders and spring training. My grandmother had a unique brand of succor; basically, it was yelling. She may have thought that her vituperative diatribes against my father consoled my mother, confirming her own worst fears and therefore, in a way, conquering them. Or perhaps she didn't intend to console my mother at all but simply to upbraid her, to pay her daughter back for marrying my father. At every opportunity, my grandmother chastised my mother for getting herself into the predicament that she was in. Her denunciations were invariably summarized by a heedless denigration of my father, then a prayer to Jude, the patron saint of lost causes.

My grandfather, on the other hand, was less critical, if for no other reason than his arteries were as constricted as a Catholic's libido and he was barely aware of the fact that he existed. He had suffered several strokes once he passed the age of fifty-five and now was kept alive by a series of pumps and clocks and stabilizers, his metabolism as mechanical as the Tin Man's. He was a marvelous specimen of the will to live, though, even if he couldn't actually be used as a poster boy for rational thought. He was gentle and, if he hadn't constantly babbled, blurting out non sequiturs to some unseen audience, he might have emanated the serene and ineffable tranquility of a tree. But he was running on sixty volts, his favorite hospital equipping him with a surgically installed piece of electronic hardware—its job to initiate involuntary muscle contractions, such as digestion—during his last anatomical pit-stop. The doctors had told my grandmother that the most important thing for her to do was to make certain that my grandfather's power supply was never interrupted. Every other day she had to change his batteries, being careful not to overcharge him when he was plugged into an AC outlet, regenerating his power pack. Plug him in and he talked. It was more like having a radio than a husband.

After I finished the dishes, I poured myself another glass of chocolate milk, took a bag of potato chips from the junk food shelf in the pantry closet, and told Rudy to come into the living room with me. Our television set was a console model the size of a stove, hulking and grim-faced when it was off. The top half was the television, the bottom contained a hi-fi system. The sound for both was channelled through the same small speaker and on the rare occasions that my mother or father played music it sounded as if it were coming through a tin can. Fine as a safety pin, the hi-fi's needle had not been changed the entire time we owned the set. To my parents, tweeters and woofers were sounds birds and dogs made, and our house was either stultifyingly silent, almost lifeless, or plagued by the cloying soundtracks of TV melodramas and the metallic clatter of canned laughter. The picture tube was on its last legs, according to my father, and required at least three minutes to "warm up" before the picture appeared. Rudy laid himself out on the floor and began drawing. I turned on the set, then sat down and began picking at the potato chips, washing them down with the chalky sludge of cheap chocolate drink. When the picture appeared, Daffy duck was pestering Elmer Fudd, who had captured Daffy, intending to cook him for his holiday dinner. But once inside Fudd's pedestrian nest, Daffy escaped and ran amuck, throwing Elmer's household into chaos before he was finally recaptured. Feigning unconsciousness, Daffy opened one eye, sized up his situation, and slipped out of the room, substituting a rubber duck for himself. He proceeded once again to turn Elmer's house into a shambles, then fled the parochial burgh, hooting insanely.

During "The Little Rascals," my grandparents arrived. My grandmother kissed Rudy and me as my grandfather took a seat on the couch, still wearing his coat and hat.

"Tom, take your coat off," my grandmother said to him.

"I've made thousands of coats," he said, remaining seated. "Hundreds even."

"I didn't ask you how many coats. God, give me the strength." My grandmother turned to me. "Where's your mother?" she said.

"Upstairs, sleeping."

"What is she doing sleeping at a time like this? How can she go to sleep?" She began climbing the stairs, muttering to her favorite saints, and using the banister railing to haul her barrel-shaped body up the steps.

My grandfather was silent. He sat perfectly erect in a corner of the sofa, propped up like a mannequin. Sometimes he went off like that, just vegged out in mid-heartbeat like he'd died. With Rudy lying silently on the floor and my grandfather as placid as a telephone pole, I felt as if I had been sucked into some weird out-of-body experience, a fourth dimension, some sort of waiting room limbo. The television droned on and after ten minutes had passed my grandmother came back downstairs, bringing with her the familiar and reorienting gift of complaint.

"What's up?"I asked.

"What's up? Your mother's in bed," she said. "That's what's up." She hung her coat, which she had carried all the way upstairs, in the closet, then took my grandfather's hat off, removed his coat, and put them in the closet beside hers. When she finished, she smoothed the front of her dress, then looked up and noticed Rudy. "Why is he undressed?" she asked me.

"You're just noticing?"

"What do I have, eyes in the back of my head? Why is he undressed? Did he come down like that?"

"No, he came down dressed and I pulled his pants off and hid them."

"Don't get smart. Did your mother see him like this?"

"I don't know."

"What was your mother going to let him do, walk around like that all day?" She was already on her way up the stairs again. "She thinks she can lie around in bed while I run her life," she said, loud enough, I was certain, for my mother to hear.

"The Little Rascals" ended and a religious talk show came on. It had been taped in the living room of a ranch-style home, the camera closing in from prairie, to corral, to three car garage, then leaping with a splice of celluloid into a mock-living room decorated with plastic plants and crucifixes. In the center of the set was a sectional sofa laid out in the shape of a cross and, in the background, a woodburning fireplace glowed softly. A choir, identified as the Leggett family singers, belted out a catchy hymn. Then there was a car commercial. When the show rematerialized, the camera slowly panned the living room and came to rest when the host appeared. He was seated at a desk and was wearing a plaid sports shirt, a string tie, and a checked jacket. He looked like a test pattern with glasses. "Good day, friends," he began, then told stories of healings and miraculous cures, of depravity and resurrection. Then he took phone calls and advised people on purchasing real estate. I got up to change channels and noticed that my grandfather was staring at the set through his magnifying glass.

"Would you like to watch anything?" I asked him.

He thought—or seemed to think—for a moment, then said, "Absolutely. 'Ed Sullivan.'"

"He's not on. It's ten o'clock in the morning," I said, expecting him to grasp the concepts of time, hours, and television programming. "Pick something else."

A longer pause this time. "'Lawrence Welk.'"

"That's a nighttime show. Night is when it's dark, like the inside of your head. Is it dark out?" I gestured toward the windows and his eyes followed my hand. I waited. "You have to think about it?" I said, imagining every on-off switch in his head stuck on "off" and painted over with stucco.

"No."

"Good. Then what is it out? Light or dark?"

He hesitated a moment.

"Now!"

"Light."

"Good. Then if it's not dark, it's not night. And if it's not night, 'Lawrence Welk' isn't on. Got that?"

"Absolutely," he said. "I have a lot of things."

"Good," I said, then began switching channels.

My grandmother came down the stairs, carrying

clothes for Rudy. She knelt on the floor beside him and motioned for Rudy to stand up when he looked at her. "Come on, sweetheart. Time to get dressed," she said, a lilt in her voice, as if she had to make clear to Rudy the good-natured intentions she had so as not to frighten him. Rudy stared at her like a cat. "Come on," she said again.

I was standing by the television set. "Rudy, get up," I said. Finding something which seemed watchable, I let go of the channel selector knob and turned around. Rudy was getting to his feet in front of my grandmother.

"Why doesn't he listen to me?" she said.

"You don't have the touch," I said. "He thinks you're a social worker."

"Oh, go away," she said.

When I moved away from the television, my grandfather said, "That's not Lawrence Welk."

A quiz show was on. "We just went through this. I told you, it's not on now."

"Michael, what are you shouting for?" my grandmother said.

"He thinks Lawrence Welk is on."

"Tom, it's ten o'clock in the morning. How could it be Lawrence Welk?"

"How should I know?"

"I'm changing the channel," I said. I flipped around and found "Jeopardy."

"That's also not Lawrence Welk," he said.

"Lawrence Welk isn't on now!" my grandmother and I shouted at him in unison.

"This is not Lawrence Welk," I said, indicating the screen. Then I realized that we all agreed. We agreed but we were arguing anyway. It was as if some gene-encoded irritability and non-comprehension sprung up every time we were put in a room together. I gave up and sat down.

My grandmother went back to dressing Rudy. She made him balance himself by placing his hand on her shoulder while he stepped into his pants. "It's all right, sweetheart," she said. "Put your hand on Nanny's shoulder." She held the trousers open for him. They were slightly large on him, having been given to my mother by someone whose son had outgrown them. The trousers were too long for Rudy and my grandmother turned the bottoms up into cuffs. She slipped his arms into the sleeves of a flannel shirt, then buttoned it. Looking at Rudy eye to eye she said, "Now, see how handsome you look." She brushed his hair with her fingers, trying to get it to go in one general direction, but it sprang back, standing up in short, prickly tufts like a brush.

As I was watching "Jeopardy," I discovered that I knew nothing about medicine, geography, history, science, and famous quotations. The only questions I could answer were about movies, trivial bits of pop culture and the names of minor TV characters. The more answers I got wrong, the more diligently I ate, filling myself with potato chips. There was no chance of me getting into medical school, certain to be a blow to my mother. It seemed I had been systematically idiotized, reduced to the level of moron by my relentless television watching. Ignorant in every area but prime time programming and syndicated reruns, I would have to list Ben Casey and Dr. Kildare as references on my medical school applications if I wanted to have a prayer of getting in.

After my grandmother had finished dressing him, Rudy lay down on the floor and picked up his pencil again. "Who drew this nice picture?" my grandmother said, leaning over him and pointing to his pad. "Did you draw it?"

Rudy didn't answer. He stopped drawing and turned his head slightly toward her, his eyes seemingly fixed on the floor and wary as an orphan's.

"Isn't this nice?" she said. "Don't you want to show it to grandpa? Go ahead, show him. No? OK, I'll show him. Grandpa, isn't this a nice picture that Rudy drew?"

My grandfather took the pad from my grandmother's hand and studied the picture. There were times when he functioned coherently, his thoughts and actions synchronized with the world around him. That this state came and went made me wonder whether or not he controlled it and used the appearance of senility as a buffer, something to keep the world at bay, or if, like a car radio, it was merely a matter of lousy reception.

"This is nice," he said. "What is it?"

He turned the pad slightly so that I could see it. Rudy had drawn a house. A primitive looking structure, it was simply a box with four smaller boxes drawn within it and split into quarters to represent windows. A rectangular box at the bottom and center of the house had a dot midway up its right hand side, representing the front door and its knob. There was no chimney. A gigantic creature looming over the house approached from behind. It had human features, but they seemed distorted—twisted, pained, and enraged. As far as I could tell, the thing was not wearing clothes, and was sexless.

"It's a monster approaching a house," I said.

My grandfather studied the drawing for a few moments, then said, "That's one way of looking at it, I suppose," and handed the pad back to Rudy, who took it from him warily.

"What do you mean, that's one way of looking at it? It's a monster attacking a house."

"Before you said approaching."

"So what? He snaps out of his trance and he's Joe Grammar."

"Tom," my grandmother said to him, "what difference does it make what he said? Tell Rudy he drew a nice picture."

"What's so nice about it?" I said. "It looks like it was drawn by a moron."

"That's not a nice thing to say."

"So what? It's a stupid picture and a stupid conversation. This whole house is stupid."

"Tom, will you tell him you're sorry. And you," my grandmother said to me, "tell your brother you're sorry for what you said."

My grandfather apologized to me with an automatic readiness. "I'm sorry if I hurt your feelings," he said.

"Forget it."

He looked at my grandmother. "Why am I apologizing?" he said.

"You see," I said. "He's a mental defective."

"Both of you stop it. I haven't got enough to do without the two of you arguing," my grandmother said. "Michael, apologize to your borther."

"Rudy, I'm sorry. You're not a moron. You're just close."

The telephone rang as I was standing there, looking at Rudy, and my grandmother, damning our lot once again, rose, saying that she would answer it. Rudy was lying on the floor again, the pencil in his hand lightly scratching the pad, moving with no sense of purpose or design. The tips of his scuffed black shoes were motionless on the carpet, his legs not kicking thoughtlessly as they sometimes did while he played. The TV was babbling away, the game show host offering a bounty of domestic gifts, and I felt slovenly and depraved, as if the glutted inanity of the tube fed the sense of desperation in me, and in our house. Of us all, Rudy was the one who least deserved my spite, and I despised myself for giving in helplessly, and with a self-appeasing malice, to my own meanness. I tapped the sole of Rudy's shoe with my foot and he turned his head and looked up at me. "I'm an idiot," I said. "I'm sorry." He looked at me blankly, and I knew that, for the moment, there was nothing more to say.

I could hear my grandmother speaking to whoever had called and I turned and walked toward the kitchen. "As far as I know he left for work," she said. "Maybe he was a little late." She paused and listened. "No. I'm just watching the children for my daughter while she's at the doctor." She was silent for a few moments again, the polish of her lies subtly unsettling, as if she had given in to this as a way of life. "I don't know," she said. "She'll be back later. Yes, I'll tell her. I'm sure he'll be there shortly. Yes," she said. "Goodbye." I was standing in the doorway when she hung up. "That was your father's boss," she said to me.

I felt myself silently withdrawing from her, from the situation, and did not answer. I sensed the world closing in around us, its subtle and indifferent malice exerting an increasing pressure on the lies we told in order to keep it at bay. Though I sensed the world closing in and around us and threatening the lies which supported our world.

At noon, the police came to our door. They had

found my father, they said, unconscious and slumped forward against the wheel of our car.

"Get your mother," my grandmother said. "Tell her they've found your father."

I bolted up the stairs two at a time and was in my mother's bedroom before I had time to take another breath.

CHAPTER FOUR

I woke my mother, told her who was downstairs, then went into my room and quickly dressed. When I came back downstairs, I found that the police were about to take my mother to the hospital where my father was being treated.

"What are you doing?" my mother asked as I was putting my jacket on.

"Going with you."

"Who's going to watch Rudy and your grandfather?"

"Nan."

"She's coming with me."

"Why?"

"Your mother's a nervous wreck," my grandmother said. "You think she can get your father home alone?"

"If she's a wreck, why are you going with her?"

"You're staying home," my grandmother said to me.

"No, I'm not."

"Can we just go, please?" one of the cops said.

"Oh, please, let's just go," my mother said.

"Can your father take care of himself while you're gone?" the other cop said to my mother.

"Yes," I said.

"You be quiet," my grandmother said. "Tom, do you feel all right?"

"I feel fine."

"Will you be all right if I leave you here alone for a little while with Rudy?"

"I ran a factory with sixty-something employees for thirty years," he said. "I think it was sixty-three."

This was as close to an answer as we were going to get from my grandfather. We took it. He and Rudy stayed home, and the rest of us left in the squad car.

My father had been taken to Redemption Hospital where he was being treated and held. He had run our car into a telephone pole and split open the bridge of his nose, according to the report that the police had.

"How did he do that?" my grandmother asked.

The cop sitting in the front passenger seat looked out the window. "Maybe he cut himself shaving," he said.

His partner shook his head. "He was doing about sixty when he hit the pole," he said to us. "He's lucky he's alive."

We had to search the car for any belongings before going to the hospital to have my father released. The site of the accident—an intersection surrounded by filling stations, bars, discount carpet warehouses, and beauty parlors, everything about the area tawdry and run-down—was crawling with tow truck operators, passersby who stopped to speculate about the wreck, and a small gathering of policemen who were standing in a circle and, from what I could make out, talking about tits. The policemen who had driven us to the spot needed to ask my mother some questions so they could make out their report. While they talked, I walked over to the car to look over the wreckage.

The car's front end had been pushed in and up, like snow which has been plowed into a pile. It was just a heap of metal, twisted and creased, a photograph of the instant the accident ended. The headlights had been smashed and there were two pools of glass scattered on the ground. The windshield was shattered but in place, a hole the size of an orange directly over the steering wheel. The front end of the car was on the sidewalk in front of a gas station. There had been no damage done to any other cars or property, and no one besides my father had been hurt. I peered inside the car window and saw that the apex of the steering wheel was cracked, and dappled with spots of dried blood. Beer cans, an empty Jack Daniels bottle, cigarette butts, and maps which had fallen out of the glove compartment—the door of which was still hanging open—littered the floor of the car. My father's necktie was on the backseat, and beside it, as if he'd been undressed at some point during the night, his undershirt.

A voice behind me said, "This fucking guy bought it, huh?"

I turned to see who was speaking. It was one of the tow truck drivers, talking to the cop who had driven out to the scene with us.

"Nah, just a busted nose," he said.

"You gotta be fucking kidding me. Are you kidding me?"

"Maybe it was all those fucking saints on the dashboard."

The policeman who was talking to my mother finished making out his report and was ready to take us to the hospital. "Is there anything here you want?" he asked my mother.

"No," she said, staring at the car.

"You're sure?" my grandmother said.

My mother was silent, and a moment later we climbed into the squad car and left.

When we arrived at the hospital, we were told that my father had escaped. He had run out of the emergency room, which was where we were standing, and disappeared. The two policemen who had brought him in and were waiting to book him for drunk driving had been unable to catch him.

"Some asshole intern let him go while we were getting coffee," one of them said.

"Well, where did he go?" my grandmother asked.

We all looked at her, a collective incredulity turning each head in the circle.

In the emergency room's lobby, orderlies were setting chairs which had been knocked over upright, and collecting papers which were strewn across the floor. The new set of cops said that when my father ran out he knocked over empty chairs and threw wire baskets filled with admissions records off the desk. He also stole a stack of invoices.

"You mean he stole bills?" my mother said.

"That's what it looks like."

"It's definitely him," I said.

I looked around at the people awaiting treatment. A large black woman was holding her right wrist with her left hand. Stuck through it like one of those arrow-through-the-head props was a twelve inch knitting needle. A man in one corner had one palm pressed to his forehead, blood dripping like beads of sweat from his brow. Beside him, a passed out teenager was covered with dried vomit and blood. A small boy, probably about Rudy's age but with the face of an old man, was bruised on the face and arms. He sat on his mother's knee as the woman stared at the floor. When she put her hand on the back of his neck and stroked it, the boy began to cry, putting his head in the crook of her neck.

My mother went and spoke to the doctor who had treated my father and, as there was nothing else that we could do, we got back into the car and left. The doctor had told my mother that my father had a broken nose and a hairline skull fracture. The three of us—my mother, grandmother, and I—sat in the backseat of the car, wrestling with our anxieties in silence. Occasionally, messages issuing from the police-band radio interrupted my thoughts about where the events of the past day were leading us. As the dispatcher droned on through the static, reporting crimes being committed in various sectors of the city, the two policemen in the front seat chatted, oblivious—or perhaps immune to—the general chaos of the place. My grandmother made plans to sleep at our house that night, talking to my mother as I stared out the window. The passivity of simply riding in a car and watching people and places go by temporarily soothed me. I had thought the situation would have been resolved, that my father would have been coming home with us by this point. As he wasn't, it felt good to simply drift.

When we arrived home and stepped out of the squad car, I noticed that a single slat of each set of venetian blinds was raised in the windows of the neighboring houses. The police drove away and as we walked toward our house I looked around again. The thin black lines stared mutely, and as my mother opened the door and entered—home to wait for word of my father—the slats were slowly lowered into alignment, the simultaneity of execution signalling a collective rebuke. I went into the house behind my mother and grandmother, then locked the door behind us.

Inside, Rudy and my grandfather were carrying on with the lucid and mechanized detachment of schizophrenics. My grandfather was pacing around the room, recounting—possibly to Rudy, although he seemed to be addressing another of his coterie of invisible friends—his adventures in the garment trade. Rudy was lying on the floor where we had left him, not quite entranced by our grandfather's tales of entrepreneurial intrigue.

"This is not the cloth I ordered," my grandfather shouted. He had one hand to the side of his head and seemed to be talking on a telephone.

"Tom, who are you talking to?" my grandmother yelled back at him.

"Leo."

"Leo's been dead for thirty years."

"Then why is he still sending me invoices?"

My grandmother held her head and groaned, before maneuvering my grandfather into a chair and calming him down.

I walked over to Rudy and looked down at what he was drawing. Covering the sheet of his pad were stick figures running within, yet seemingly unable to escape from the confines of rhombuses and trapezoids, their pursuers anonymous, their terror mute. I saw for the first time that Rudy viewed existence as a terror-ridden term of imprisonment. His vision, juxtaposed with my grandfather's incarceration in senility, suddenly revealed to me in a way I could feel but not fully understand, the paradoxical dread and absurdity of existence. I wanted to reach down and stroke Rudy's head, calm him as I would a startled and wary animal. But, at that moment, I was afraid to. I was ashamed, after all those years, to risk making a connection and having it fail. Or worse, to be rejected. And so I retreated, once more, into myself, when Rudy raised his eyes and looked up at me, as if for an answer.

My mother was sitting in the armchair, holding a crumpled handkerchief in her hand.

"Do you see what your husband's doing to us?" my grandmother said, hanging up her coat. "If he shows up here, he's going to have the cops on him. I'll tell you that right now."

"Who says he's coming home?" my mother said.

"Where else does he always go when he's done drinking? You think some tootsie is going to put up with his nonsense? She'd throw him out on his ear."

My grandfather got up from the sofa. "I'm going to Brooklyn," he said.

"Tom," my grandmother yelled, "will you sit down and be quiet?" shoving him back down onto the couch. He fell silent again, turning one palm up in the air as if dismissing his efforts as futile to some unseen party.

I started up the stairs.

"Where are you going?" my grandmother said.

"To my room."

"What for?"

"I want to."

"What's the matter? You can't stay with your family? All you think about is yourself. What about how we feel?"

I continued up the steps and didn't answer.

CHAPTER FIVE

Late in the afternoon, as we were eating the dinner my grandmother had prepared for us, the telephone rang. It was my father's boss again, wanting to know where his star employee had been that day. My mother told him that my father had been in an accident driving to work and that he'd been taken to the hospital for treatment. There hadn't been time to call the office. I could tell by the information my mother began feeding the man that his tone had changed, became solicitous and consoling, rather than aggressive and, I'm sure, vaguely threatening.

"He's not too bad," my mother said. "He has a broken nose and a concussion." There was a pause. "No, no, he's not in the hospital. He's upstairs in bed, resting."

For some time I had known that my mother addressed the truth of our situation equivocally—fantasizing about out prospects, glossing over the dispiriting shambles of our life—but I did not remember ever hearing her tell an out-and-out lie before. She'd always qualified her deviations from the strict truth by adding, "if all goes well," or something like that. It was self-deception rather than deceit in that what she said bore no relation to the real world, only to her own. But now she had lied, and she saw that I was stunned.

"Yes, I know," she said, getting up from her seat and taking the phone into the darkened dining room. "I've been telling him for weeks that the brakes needed to be looked at, but he was always too busy," she continued. "The doctor says we're lucky to have him alive." My mother was silent for a few moments. "Yes, I suppose he does have a lot of things on his mind. Yes, I know that lately he's been much better."

My father's boss liked my father, and had since the day he'd hired him. He was an Irishman, like my father, and when my father—con man that he was—interviewed for the trainee position, he told his future boss that he was living at home and taking care of his Irish mother. Typing? No problem. He had picked that up in the Marines. This must have been the only time in his life that my father used the word type when he wasn't referring to a girl as not his . . . I am certain that my father had never even sat in front of a typewriter, let alone touched the keys. But the old Irishman who interviewed him ignored the possibility that my father might have been lying and hired him—for mom, the flag, and blarney—without even administering a test.

"It isn't easy raising a family," my mother said, "and he tries so hard. He's so eager to get ahead." At this point we completely leaped the tracks of reality, my mother attempting the mind-boggling, even the heroic: trying to turn a call announcing my father's termination into a testimony to his skills, dedication, and underappreciated efforts. There was a warped bravery in her persistence, and a good deal of flat-out insanity. She was silent again, then said, "Certainly, Bill. I'll call to let you know how he's doing. I'll tell him that you called. Yes. OK. Goodnight." My mother came back into the kitchen and hung up the telephone. We were all silent—my grandmother and I consciously, Rudy and my grandfather from habit and obliviousness. I watched my mother as she sat down at the table. She picked up her fork, but only to have something to hold on to; she didn't attempt to eat. She didn't—or wouldn't—look at any of us. As she sat there, the anxiety she was hiding seemed to turn into something tangible. It began to change the lines of her face and I knew that she felt she'd disgraced herself. It was no longer a matter of simple self-deception; she had used someone else, lied to them in order to preserve her own world, even better it. And she understood this, was aware of what she had done, and this knowledge admitted the real world—with all its pitiless momentum—into her own. I believe it was then that she began to sense things coming to an end, things which had existed in her words alone, and slowly, releasing herself—or unable to restrain herself from it—she began to cry, filled with the knowledge of her own shame. The rest of us were silent, each of us perhaps feeling the same sadness for my mother that the others felt. Though she had duped my father's boss, his earnest response had left her, in a way, more defenseless than if he had challenged her lies. Instead, she had been left alone with her sins, defending them now only to herself. As I watched her, I knew that I was seeing my mother's dreams end. The creeping facticity of the world, moving with tortoise-like determination, had inched its way past her static and ultimately insupportable illusions, illusions which had their genesis in the same office which now seemed capable of ending them.

The office itself was drab and small. The walls were yellowing with age. The windows looking out onto the airshafts and the street were clouded with a greyish film of dirt, and the tile floor was scuffed and cracking. It had the mark of a place which has been overused and forgotten. There were only a dozen people who worked there, all in clerical positions of varying degree. Except for my father, the men were all middle-aged. His boss was a paunchy, red-faced Irishman with nicotine-stained fingertips and short, bristly hair the color of a dime. He ran the office, which was the New York branch of a freight-forwarding company, with a mixture of irritable sternness and garrulous good will that depended on his mood. The men were the various managers and assistant managers, and the women the secretaries. A few of them shuffled around the office in slippers, the arches of which had been flattened by years of wear. Veterans of both the Depression and the War, they clung tenaciously to their jobs. Only one of the men had a college degree. The rest, like my father, had begun at the bottom and—with no other prospects—simply hung on, the fear that they might have had no job at all lowering their expectations. My father often complained that no one understood why he was bored with the job, or anxious to move up or—better yet—out. In his own frustration, he mocked the paltry thrift of his co-workers. Saving for retirement, they wore resoled shoes and carried liverwurst and wilted lettuce sandwiches to work in paper bags. The present was dead to them, he raved. They were all sheep, accepting their lot without the dignity of raging against the unfairness of it, its unsuitability and disgrace. All they wanted, he said, was the possibility of a few years of peace, and then the grave.

None of this hangdog resignation suited my father. His first Christmas in the office, there was a party, as always. Everyone worked until noon, then the women put food out on the desks. One by one they lined up, filled their plates, and ate in virtual silence, a few of them commenting on the dishes the women had prepared, or noting how quickly the year had passed. My father was waiting for the liquor to come out, and told everyone who encouraged him to eat that he would in a minute. Finally, the manager opened a bottle of rye and some of the men mixed drinks. There was a toast, everyone raised their glasses, took a sip of their drinks, then cleaned up and went home. Only half of the rye had been poured out. My father helped clear the paper plates off the desks, organized a few papers on his own, and, dragging behind in order to be the last one out of the office, grabbed the bottle of rye and slipped it inside his coat pocket. He started his own Christmas party which lasted three days.

He was the assistant-assistant manager in a department of three. Nothing short of the death of one of his bosses would bring him a promotion. But he was unconcerned with this, he later told me. The job represented a paycheck; was stop-gap, temporary, a place to perch while he figured out where he wanted to go next. In the end—we can jump ahead now, why not?—he stayed thirty-four years. Some perch.

When she first met him, my mother expected my father to go places, too. What she learned was that he didn't want to take her. She was one of the office secretaries, a graduate of the John Hancock School of Clerical Arts. Skilled in typing and stenography, she had not finished high school, seeing no reason to as she planned to marry money. My grandfather had done well, handsomely in fact, in the coat manufacturing business. Then he invested in an Italian electronics company and they took him to the cleaners. A few hospital bills later, he was wiped out. But my mother had grown up with the comforts of wealth, and she was, in some way, incapable of accepting the fact that those luxuries no longer existed. She believed that all you had to do was want something enough and it would come.

At ten o'clock each morning my mother appeared at my father's desk and asked him, as she asked everyone else in the office, if he would like anything from the coffee shop downstairs. He said yes—always. Coffee—tons of sugar—and a danish. She waited for him to give her some money, but he always said, "I'll get you when you get back." This was her first mistake: she trusted him. After all, he wore expensive suits which had been dry cleaned and pressed, unlike the other men whose outfits seemed to have been preserved in mothball-filled trunks since the time of their high school graduations. Whenever she returned, he was nowhere near his desk. Everyone else paid her, unwrapped their sweets, and went back to work. Meanwhile, she stood at the new assistant-assistant-manager's desk, waiting for him. Five minutes after she'd given up and left his breakfast, he'd return. Second mistake: she believed this was a coincidence—even though it happened every morning for the first few days. Or, perhaps, she wanted to believe that it was a coincidence, some Hollywood version of the "cute meet" trickling down to the world of deskbound mortals. Nevertheless, she was always too embarrassed to ask him for the money he owed her, and the few times he offered to pay her—tomorrow, of course—she said to forget it. And he did. A few weeks later, they began dating.

My mother thought my father had money. He lived in Manhattan, wore expensive suits, and carried himself with a sense of self-assurance that could only come from great wealth, or else deluded grandeur not yet tended to by mood stabilizers and serious psychiatric counseling. What she didn't know was that he lived in a cold water flat with his mother and sister. My father, on the other hand, believed that my mother was rich, after hearing her tell of the house in Queens, the trips to Florida, and the manufacturing business that her father had run. Each of them had the impression that they were getting someone else, and the momentum of that early infatuation—combined with the unquestioning force of lust—quickened their thoughts until it was as if decisions were being made for them, completely beyond their control.

Three months after they met, my parents were engaged.

"Oh, yeah. You got engaged tonight?" the bartender at Kinelly's said to my mother. "Congratulations." She and my father had gone out to celebrate. Kinelly's was my father's favorite gin mill, also one of the most generous toward him. At the time of the engagement, he owed Kinelly's over three hundred 1947 dollars. "Who's the guy?" the bartender asked. My mother pointed out my father. He was shooting pool with his old cronies, Baldy Fitzgerald and Trigger Dillon, neighborhood boys from the Irish section of the Upper West Side. It was the first time my mother had been in a bar. She came from a large Italian family, and when they celebrated they ate, talked, and played cards, but did very little drinking. Just some wine with dinner. Women in the family rarely, if ever, drank, and the act itself was considered somehow shabby, and tainted. Definitely lower class. An insular family, not immune to the dubious codes of respect espoused by the Mafia, they did not readily accept strangers into their midst, and looked down upon anyone who spent time in bars.

"Where?" the bartender said. "You're pointing to the men's room."

"No. There. That's my fiancé."

The bartender looked again. "McManus? You got engaged to that nut job?"

"Yes," my mother said, looking back at the bartender. "What's wrong with that?"

"Lady, all I can say is—good luck."

They had spent the afternoon downtown on Canal Street, picking out the engagement ring, paying for it with borrowed cash, then going uptown to show it off to my father's friends. "One drink," my father had said. At midnight, they were looking for a cab, my mother stuck with an eight dollar fare for taking her back to Queens.

My grandmother instantly hated my father. The first time he was introduced to the family was at a party at my grandparents' house. His forehead was bandaged, covering a gash over his left eye. As my mother led him into the large dining room, the boisterous talking and mock threats the men made in jest ceased. Every eye in the room was on him.

"This is who you're marrying?" my grandmother said in the kitchen. "He looks like a maniac."

"He hit his head getting out of a cab," my mother said, which is what my father had told her he'd done. Actually he'd cut it in a barroom fight the night before.

My grandfather, then still coherent, said to her, "What was it, moving?"

My mother and grandmother argued, my grandmother insisting that my mother no longer see my father. A week later, they were engaged. Three months after that, they were married.

They honeymooned in upstate New York. During the day, my father shunned all social activity—the archery, the shuffleboard, the organized hiking. But by late afternoon he was arranging parties at their rented cottage. Guests brought bottles of liquor, as my father had casually suggested. He supplied ice and glasses, which, of course, he had taken from the retreat's recreation room, then cajoled the other couples into feeding quarters into the radio so that they'd have some music. People danced and got drunk, then left. The following morning my father would turn the radio upside down and shake all the quarters out of it.

"I don't think you should do that," my mother said, a bit surprised, I imagine, at seeing my father turn into a petty thief on their honeymoon.

"Don't worry," my father told her. "This is perfectly legal. Trust me."

Each morning before breakfast, my mother once told me, they made love. My mother had been a virgin when they married and it was painful when my father entered her, even after the first few times. What my mother had preserved for twenty-one years my father negated within seconds after arriving at the hotel suite the night of the wedding. Every morning he matched his post-nuptial haste as if trying to break a record, like some sprinter. He was unaffectionate, hurrying in a way which made her think he was disgusted by sex, and she began, very quickly, to find the whole process cold and mechanical. By the end of the week my mother knew that it was definitely not love, but there was nothing she could do. She was married to him, had an apartment on the top floor of my grandparents' house waiting for them, and hundreds of dollars worth of unopened wedding gifts sitting on its floors. And they had me. Within a fortnight of the wedding, I had been conceived.

My father had a rough time adjusting to married life. He stayed out all night a few times a week, occasionally forgetting where he lived and calling home from a phone booth in Manhattan. After several nights of sitting up with her pregnant daughter, my grandmother convinced my grandfather that he should have a talk with his wayward son-in-law. So he did. My father explained that he didn't come directly home after work because he liked to have an evening cocktail.

"For three days?" my grandfather said.

"That's a fuck-up, no question. I admit that. But look at the big picture."

So my grandfather looked while my father painted. A. He worked hard and was entitled to a drink—always with my father it was a drink, one drink. B. My mother didn't like him drinking at home. C. What choice did he have but to have his drink somewhere else. Warily, my grandfather decreed that my father had the right to drink in his own house.

"I'm saying one drink," my grandfather told him.

"Absolutely."

"I'm trusting you. Don't let me down."

"Don't worry. No chance."

And so my father began spending evenings at home. Sitting in my grandparents' living room, he would make small talk while demurely sipping his drink. Every thirty minutes or so he would excuse himself and run up to his apartment to take a slug from a bottle in his own stock, or slip into the bathroom and take a hit from the flask he carried discreetly in his back pocket. After several trips, he actually began to enjoy the coziness of married life. And by the end of some of those many mellow nights, he even thought—as he lay in bed watching the late movie, my mother, pregnant with me, having accommodated him during his brief lust, by then asleep—that being married was not so terrible after all. Amazingly enough, he was nearly content.

About the time I was born, his restlessness set in again, and the binges began. He was not cut out to be a father, not at that age, and, unfinished and frustrated, he considered me one more trap in his life. He threatened to leave my mother, but never did; lost his old friends but made no new ones; and slowly, a loner in many ways his whole life, slipped more and more deeply into himself. Once, after he had been drinking, I somehow caught his attention and he began playing with me, tossing me up into the air and catching me in his large hands. My mother came into the room, saw what he was doing, and told him to be careful. My father took this to mean, don't touch him, and his isolation was complete. My parents fought and remained together. My mother cried and my grandmother reminded her that she had said that my father was no good. Every time the situation became intolerable and it was decided that something should be done, nothing was. The only solution was unacceptable. No divorce, my grandmother ruled. And so my mother, who could not break away on her own, and my father, who always returned to us, unable to break away himself, remained together.

Nature played its hand. The assistant manager in my father's department died and my father was promoted. He had managed, in spite of his drinking—and in part because of his need to continue drinking—to hold onto his job. It supported his habit and, marginally, his family, thereby mitigating any minor guilt he may have felt. With the promotion, my mother saw some light ahead, and began planning for the future again, trying to reinforce in my father the idea that he was intelligent and could be a success if he applied himself. He began to take himself more seriously and told my mother about an idea he had that could mean a savings for the company. On her advice, he wrote it down and dropped it into the suggestion box in the office. The main office in Chicago thought the idea was valid and cost-effective, and awarded my father a bonus of four hundred dollars. On the basis of this success, it was decided that what would be best for us was a house of our own. So, my grandparents lent my parents the money for the downpayment and my parents bought a place around the corner from where we had lived. The future suddenly seemed to hold some promise and, with the encouragement of my mother's cousin, who was a priest, my father agreed to go away on a retreat. When he returned he was full of ideas and resolutions. Then my mother told him that she was pregnant with Rudy, and his plans for saving enough money to start his own business were sucked into the abyss of unrealized ambitions—baby food, diapers, and doctor bills consuming every spare dollar in the house. Shortly before Rudy was born, my father brought home the company's bi-monthly newspaper. Six months earlier it had mentioned my father's suggestion and the money awarded him. The current issue reported that implementation of his idea had saved the company seven hundred and fifty thousand dollars in the previous fiscal quarter alone.

A few months after Rudy's birth, my father's mother came to stay with us. We rarely saw her, as she lived with my father's sister. We were virtually strangers, linked to one another by blood only. She felt foreign to me, unfamiliar in a way my other grandparents were not. Thin, her hands as gnarled as the roots of a tree by arthritis, short gray whiskers sprouting from her chin, she seemed hag-like and—though I didn't want to admit it—vaguely frightening. My aversion to her did not go unnoticed by my father, and I could tell that he resented me for it. He was uncomfortable around his mother. Unaffectionate, nervously awkward, he tried to make sure she was happy the entire time she was with us. I am certain that she was as uneasy as we were. There was a ready smile on her lips at all times, and an alert effort to be inconspicuous and polite. My mother tried to make her feel welcome, but the results were clumsy and superficial. By the middle of the week my father began stopping at the corner bar for a bracer as he was coming home from work, and at the end of the uneasy week we all rode out to New Jersey to bring my grandmother back home. Driving back, my mother broke the silence and said that she thought my father's mother had had a nice time.

"Just shut up," my father snapped, turning his head to glare at her.

After a few moments he looked back at the road and directed the car into one lane again. We drove in silence for a few moments, then my father pounded the dashboard with his fist and swore incoherently. He pulled up onto the shoulder of the turnpike, stopped the car, and got out. He walked away from us and out into a field bordering the road, then stood in the middle of nothing and looked down at the ground. The sun was setting and, as we waited for him to return—wondering if he was going to—he turned into a small black figure, pacing now, against an indifferent horizon. An hour later he returned and we drove home. Two weeks later, while he was hanging wallpaper in the dining room, as my mother had requested, the phone rang. His sister was calling to say that their mother was in a hospital. My mother thought that they were both going to be killed the way my father drove, racing to get to the place. His speeding did him no good. When he reached her room, his mother was dead.

After that, my father slowly returned to living the way he had driven to the hospital that night, recklessly and with no concern for any purpose but his own. The sobriety of body and spirit which had temporarily dominated him was gone and he drank regularly and heedlessly again, missing days at work, and telling my mother what she could do with her plans for renovating. One night, while we were sitting at the table eating—Rudy smearing carrot puree on his undershirt, exhibiting Fauvist inclinations early in his career—my mother mentioned that a dining room set she had been thinking about was on sale. We were broke, in debt, and would be, if we made no further purchases, until sometime after the turn of the century. But to my mother, life was for wanting.

"It's really a good buy," she said. "I think my parents will lend us the money."

"I don't give a fuck about what your parents are going to do. I don't give a fuck about a dining room set. And I don't give a fuck about what you want. What about what I want?"

The discussion ended and, in a way, so did all hope for the happy ending which seemed remotely possible. What my father wanted was never revealed, but what did become apparent was that the force which drove my parents apart, and into such unhappiness, came not from either one of them alone, but the two of them together. And yet, in spite of this, my parents remained together, eking out a life in which imagination failed, and affection proved elusive and ultimately insupportable.

My mother got up from the table, excusing herself, saying she needed to lie down and rest her eyes. She went up to her bedroom while the rest of us, in stunned silence, tried to finish dinner.

Rudy persisted in ignoring his food and my grandmother tried to coax him into eating by telling him, in a shrill, sing-song voice, to pretend that he was an inanimate object, such as an airplane hangar or a tunnel, and that what he was about to ingest was an airplane or a locomotive. Controlled by my grandmother's hand, the fork did a series of dips and curves, then banked through a one hundred eighty degree U-turn and headed for Rudy's lips. When it got there, the hangar doors were closed.

"Come on, sweetheart," my grandmother said, "you have to eat something."

"He ate this morning," I said. "He had a bite of a waffle."

"That's not enough for him to eat."

"It's about right for him, for this time of year." After observing Rudy for years, it seemed to me as if there was a pattern to his eating habits. He ate once a day during the spring and fall, and three times a week in summer and winter, sustaining himself by some weird conjunction with the seasons.

My grandmother tried once more, but met with no luck. She left Rudy alone and began clearing the dishes from the table while I helped. As I took his plate, I caught Rudy's eye and, instead of immediately averting his gaze as he usually did, he continued to look at me. Just for an instant. Then he seemed to snap out of his semi-trance and turned his eyes away from mine. I felt that I had, in some way, been thanked for understanding him, which was nothing more than simply noticing what his habits were. But perhaps this was enough.

While my grandmother did the dishes, I took my grandfather into the living room to watch the news. I pulled the rocking chair close to the set and turned it on. The reception actually seemed better when he was in the room. I imagined that, filled with metallic parts, he attracted the television signal like an antenna. But even with Walter Cronkite's head six inches away from him and large as a pumpkin, he still had to sit close to the set and hold a magnifying glass in front of his already bespectacled eyes in order to see the picture clearly. When I peered through the glass Walter Cronkite's head ballooned and curved, each eye the size of a silver dollar. I took a long sideways glance at my grandfather, who, in spite of all the visual accoutrements, was squinting. I wondered if he wasn't perhaps in the final phase of human existence, on the brink of relinquishing his human powers in order to carry on as a form of vegetable life.

I didn't know why my grandfather watched the news. He lacked the ability to absorb and order the information he received; memory was a wasted and random talent; one moment disconnected from the next for him. But perhaps this is what attracted my grandfather to the news—its porosity and flux. Events occurred, were reported, and then were swallowed up by the quicksand-like pit of information in which judgement was mired and vision overwhelmed by the enormous and haphazard accretion of facts. To one who made little sense himself, it must have seemed a perfect reflection of consciousness. Nothing added up to a final sum except the ball scores, for which I patiently waited while my grandfather absorbed the history and trivia of another day as indiscriminately as a sponge.

But Walter Cronkite did not cover events in the baseball world, I rediscovered. Though I occasionally watched a few minutes of his broadcast, I had never stayed with it until the end when the ball scores were usually given. So after he told my grandfather and me that that was the way it was on September 27, 1961, I said, "What kind of news doesn't give you the baseball scores?" My grandfather didn't answer me, as I soon realized I expected. He continued to stare at the television set as the credits rolled by, oblivious to me, the end of the news, the entire logical world around him. Without an evening paper, which I depended upon my father to bring home, I had to listen to the radio to get the results of the game. Roger Maris had not hit his sixty-first home run. Instead, he had taken the day off to get away from the pressure of the quest. I turned off the radio, went inside, and sat with my grandfather. We watched TV until it grew late, and then turned off the lights and went up to our beds to sleep.

CHAPTER SIX

The following morning I dressed for school, then went down to the kitchen to make breakfast. My mother was showering and my grandmother dressing before calling the police to see if they had any news concerning my father's whereabouts, as if they wouldn't notify us if they had. I laid cereal bowls on the table, along with several dulled, water-stained spoons. I put out Rice Crispies, Fruit Loops, Captain Crunch, and Corn Flakes, plus a quart of milk and the sugar bowl. I put a potful of water for tea on the stove and turned on the burner, then went to the front door to get the morning paper. When I came back inside, Rudy, I found, had awakened and come downstairs. He was lying on the floor, watching "Johnny Jellybean."

"How about some breakfast?" I said. Rudy kept watching the show. "OK, I'd like that," I said. "Good,

I'll make you some, Rudy." I went into the kitchen to get him a bowl of cereal.

While I was shaking Captain Crunch from the box, my grandfather came into the kitchen. He was wearing his pajamas and bathrobe and, obviously forgetting his manners—just as he'd forgotten his name, identity, and reason for being—his brown homburg. It was an understandable mistake; anyone could have made it. And so once he had seated himself, I walked around the table and removed it. Fine strands of white hair flew up from his scalp, chasing the electrical charge given off by the band of the hat. I smoothed it back down against his scalp and he seemed to respond to the attention. Then I noticed that he was wearing lace-up shoes and black socks. It was seven in the morning. I wasn't ready to deal with the futility of an inquiry, so I let it pass. I finished making Rudy's breakfast, even tossing in half a sliced banana, still hoping that his condition was due to a vitamin deficiency and was chemically correctable. My grandfather, however, was well beyond hope. I made him a cup of tea, then said, "Would you like some breakfast?"

"Great day," he said. "Truly outstanding."

I assumed that meant yes, then realized that I was the only one of the two of us who considered there to be a correlation between meaning and content in our conversations. I had begun to supply both in my dealings with Rudy and my grandfather. Without wondering if the relationships existed on a plane of pure intuition, floating out there somewhere beyond the reaches of empirical fact, or if they were indeed solely expressions of my own prejudices, I was certain that some sort of communication did exist, and that dialogues indeed occurred. I did not know, however, how either Rudy or my grandfather felt about this, or if they even suspected that we were communicating, though I believed that Rudy had initiated and somehow even controlled the flow of understanding which passed between him and myself.

I poured Corn Flakes into a yellow Boontonware cereal bowl, then prepared them according to my grandfather's traditional specifications.

"Hold this spoon," I said to him.

I filled it with maple syrup, then took it from his hand, his capacity for following instructions limited to allowing himself to be manually posed, then freezing. Once he was set up he would remain as still as a figure cast in plaster. I poured the syrup over the cereal, then went to the sink, filled the tablespoon—this time with water—and poured that over the cereal as well.

"Do you want to mix it yourself?" I asked him.

"That's enough syrup," he said, lagging somewhat behind my conversational pace.

"Great."

I tossed the flakes until they were lightly coated with the caramel-colored syrup, then slid the bowl in front of him.

"Here," I said, "and make sure you chew it this time," recalling his choking incident of the week before when he had tried to swallow his steak one lump at a time. Finally finished, I sat down, hoping to be able to read the paper without interruption.

"What is he doing with his shoes and socks on?" My grandmother had just come into the room and was obviously keen on getting an early start on nagging for the day.

"How should I know?" I said. "What did the police say?"

"What do you think they said? That that lunatic father of yours has disappeared for good for all they know."

"He's not a lunatic."

"No, this is normal that he runs away every few months. You remember the last time? He almost lost his job. You think I like explaining to everyone why your mother's always depressed, why Rudy doesn't talk?"

"What are you blaming him for?"

"Why do you stick up for him? Has he ever treated you any better than he's treated the rest of us?"

I would not admit to her that he hadn't. He had treated us all terribly; yet, I always found myself forgiving him. Something in me would never let me believe that it all was his fault. But each time I forgave him, hoping that it was the last time I would have to, he gave me, shortly afterwards, another occasion for disappointment. One rainy afternoon I had been lying on my bed, reading. Unexpectedly, my father sauntered into the room, hands in his hip pockets. When I looked up at him he smiled. I went back to my book, but out of the corner of one eye watched him. He was standing in the middle of the room looking around at the walls as if he was considering redecorating. Finally, he sat down on Rudy's bed, facing me.

"Did you have a game today?" he said.

I played on the grammar school baseball team. "We started one," I said. "It was called on account of rain." Why did he suddenly want to know, I wondered.

"Get any hits?"

"A single."

"That's good. You guys win?"

"I told you that the game was called."

"Oh, right. That's good."

Very incidentally he brought up his purpose, as if it had just occurred to him why he was there. "Listen," he said, "Mom's out for the afternoon and I'm supposed to pick up a couple of things at the hardware store." If he said he was "buying hardware" that meant he'd be drinking down in the basement for the rest of the afternoon. He kept bottles stashed up in the cross-hatchings of the ceiling, in between the X's formed by furring strips nailed to the supporting beams of the house. I had found one one day when I climbed up on a chair to get my Winchester rifle down from the top of a cabinet. Who my father thought he was fooling when he announced that he was going down into the basement to work was beyond me. He'd descend cold sober and an hour later come up plastered. Then he'd deny that he'd had anything to drink. "Anyway," he continued, "your mother didn't leave any money around the house and I gotta get some washers. Do you have any money around?"

I knew that whatever I gave him I'd never see again. "No."

"You don't have any money at all?"

"No."

"You got over fifty bucks for your communion less than two weeks ago."

"I spent it."

"Don't tell me you spent it. What did you spend it on?"

"I bought a Rocky Colavito glove."

"I know you didn't spend all of it." He rose from Rudy's bed. "Where is it?" He went to my dresser, opened the top drawer, and began scavenging among my socks and underwear. I lay on my bed holding the book I had been reading, watching him grow more and more frantic. I studied him closely, looking for any indication that he had discovered the secret purpose of the toy cannon on my dresser. Rolled cylindrically and stuffed inside its barrel were three ten dollar bills. I had six one dollar bills and some loose change in the night table drawer beside my bed, a sum I had decided would be an adequate decoy and not too dear a sacrifice to make.

My father finished going through the third drawer of my dresser, then turned toward me. "Just give me some money," he said, enunciating his words clearly, knowing that I knew that the more controlled he tried to seem, the more berserk he was on the brink of becoming.

"I've got about three dollars, all right?" I leaned over and opened the drawer beside me. I quickly grabbed three singles and turned to offer them to him. But he was already standing over me. He grabbed the drawer by its handle and yanked it out of the night table. The contents of the drawer scattered in the air and fell to the floor, coins rolling on their edges and then wobbling in circular motions before coming to rest. He plucked the three dollar bills that I had left in the drawer from the floor, then went around, stooped over, picking up the nickels and dimes. When he stood up he walked over to me. The drawer was still hanging by its handle from his left hand. He glared at me, then reached down and snatched the three dollar bills I was holding from my fist. He stuck the money into his hip pocket, looking at me as he did. I glared back at him. And though I pulled my head back when he swung, his right hand caught me on the left temple anyway, and I fell back against my pillow and, for a moment, saw double.

"Next time you'll get worse," he said.

Then he turned and left for the barroom, tossing the empty drawer into a corner of the room as he left.

"You see. You know I'm right," my grandmother said.

My mother walked into the kitchen. "What are you two shouting about?" she said. "It's seven-thirty in the morning."

"Mr. Know-It-All doesn't think his father's done anything wrong."

"I didn't say that. I said he's not a lunatic."

"Both of you, do me a favor," my mother said. "Shut up."

"Oh, now I'm going to hear it from you all day," my grandmother said to my mother.

I got up to leave.

"I'm going," I said.

"Comb your hair before you leave," my mother said.

Her command, her dictation of the rules of appearances, was so automatic that I ignored it and she instantly forgot it. I slipped on my jacket and went out the door to school.

In the yard I joined my friends, some of whom had heard stories of what supposedly had happened at my house in the past two days.

"Hey, I heard your old man cracked up the fuckin' car," Tony Calante said. "Is that true? Rinaldi said he disappeared."

"Ask Rinaldi."

"Don't get touchy. I was asking a simple question."

That's all you're capable of asking, I thought, instantly hating him for his strangeness, his directness, for his existing beyond the blood-drawn borders of familiarity.

"Really? Michael, is this true? This happened?" It was Edward Gerulitis who, despite being the school's resident genius, reacted with amazement each time he was confronted by something which actually had happened.

"No, I made it up so I wouldn't have to do my homework."

A teacher blew a whistle. The brothers lined us up and marched us into church. When Mass let out I headed for the cafeteria to pick up my second breakfast. On the way I stopped in the lavatory to relieve myself. The cold, damp, tiled room and the wall of urinals smelled of a combination of disinfectant, incense, and cigarette smoke. I found an open stall, unzipped my fly, thrust my hips forward into the hollow of the fixture, and unclenched. As I was absent-mindedly staring at the crumbling grout four inches from the tip of my nose, Patrick McGuire came up behind me and spoke into my ear.

"Radowitz is telling everybody that your old man's a drunk."

I finished peeing, zipped up my fly, flushed, and turned around. The bathroom was crowded, filled with guys milling around waiting for the fight which they knew was imminent, even before I myself had known. Radowitz was standing at the far end of the bathroom, waiting. Everyone hated Radowitz, including Radowitz. He was a weasel, an instigator, and irredeemably obnoxious. Wanting to be noticed, included, like the rest of us, he had created his personality out of the dregs of despicable behavior. He might be loathsome, but he would be acknowledged.

Everyone knew that Radowitz was totally incapable of defending himself. He was short and pudgy and when I came close to him he was biting down on his lower lip, trying to look cocky and assured. He had a strange head. It was perfectly square on the top and sides, and the lower part was long, finished off by a pouch which hung beneath his chin like a pelican's.

"You're saying stuff about my father?"

"I didn't say nothin'."

"Don't get cute. Just tell me what you said so I don't have to beat your brains in."

We were imitating movie toughs, the form of the entire encounter living somewhere in both our memories as celluloid myth.

"Fuck you," he said.

He looked around at the faces watching us and smiled. When he looked back at me I saw in that look of brute stupidity everything I wanted to destroy: my mother's insistence upon perpetuating the status quo even if it was a lie, my grandmother's self-righteous stupidity, my father's selfish and pathetic bullying of us all. Suddenly I wanted to beat Radowitz senseless for all his ignorance, for everything he thought he knew but didn't. I grabbed him by his tie and shoved him back against the wall.

"You want me to beat your brains in, don't you?"

Radowitz was gagging, but he tried to laugh, his mock bravado never deserting him.

"Kiss my ass," he said.

I stabbed my fist into his soft stomach and he coughed out air.

"Tell me what you said."

"Piss off."

I smacked his face twice, back of the hand then quickly back across his face with the palm. Radowitz laughed. I smacked him again.

"Tell me what you said."

"Fuck yourself."

I brought my knee up into his groin and he stopped breathing. I stood him up and slammed him back against the wall, then hit him again. He started to ball up but before he could I brought the palm of my hand up from my waist and smashed his forehead. His head snapped back and I heard a dull crack as it smacked against the tile wall.

"Fuck you and your whole fucking family," Radowitz yelled. And then he started to cry.

I lost control of myself. I hit him as hard as I could in the face and his nose started to bleed. I wanted to beat that brute ignorance back into silence. Someone yelled out that the back of Radowitz's head was bleeding. Then the door opened and the custodian walked in; everyone fell silent. The cheering stopped. I stopped hitting Radowitz and let him go. I was breathing hard but I could feel the deep breaths planing out inside me, coming to rest as if they were some huge dark bird landing on water.

"You prick, I hate you," Radowitz said.

I looked at him. He was the thing I hated and could not put down and I said, "Good."

"Everybody out!" the custodian shouted.

We flew like bats.

I decided not to go straight home after school. Instead, I walked up to Forest Park, a large, untended area of woods at the fringe of the neighborhood. We used the place for sledding during the winter, hundreds of kids flying down the face of places called Snake Hill and the Soup Bowl. I walked through the park past the band shell where they held concerts on the weekends, white-haired old men pumping out John Philip Sousa music for a decorous and unspirited audience, the older folks in town, like my grandfather, who had grown useless but seemed, somehow, to continue to blossom in their states of relentless tedium.

I wandered up the hill to the carousel. It had been built just before the turn of the century and the benches and horses were carved and painted in a very bright, very ornate Victorian style. The concession which sold popcorn and ice cream during the summer was boarded up for the coming winter. I climbed onto one of the horses and told it to move. The two of us remained there in a state of dumb arrest. I exhaled, then released the reins. As I sat there I remembered being on a horse on a ride called Steeplechase at Coney Island amusement park. There were lanes of track and wooden horses ran along the track, the faster ones to the left.

My grandmother took Rudy, who was no more than four at the time, and I rode a horse with my mother. We were on one of the slower ones and we took off from the gate and flew toward the precipice that was at the end of the wide field of lanes. I couldn't see anything beyond the drop; there was simply an end to it, and then sky. About halfway down the field I heard this whooping and screaming, yee-ha's, like a cowboy driving cattle. In an instant a horse sped by my mother and me to our left. The horse seemed to be flying and my father was on it, standing with his feet in the stirrups, holding the reins with one hand. One of the attendants signalled to my father to sit down. My father laughed a pretty insane laugh, something maniacally free in its heedlessness, and he raised his free hand and stuck his middle finger up at the man. Then he glanced at my mother and me, still laughing, still holding up his finger, and his laugh turned into a howl. Then his horse sped away from us and dropped, bearing my father on its back, out of sight, over the edge of the precipice. I climbed down off the horse and walked away from the carousel.

After wandering for a while without thinking where I was heading, I found myself in a heavily wooded area of the park on a long, deserted lane. Black lamp-posts with bird-cage tops were strung out along the path, their glass bulbs broken and left untended. As I walked I remembered that the area had been banned to school children because several students claimed to have been molested there by a psychotic pederast who had supposedly escaped from an insane asylum located only a few miles away. I told myself to ignore the stories. But as I walked I became convinced of the mute hostility of the woods, the pitilessness of everything around me, and the presence of some horror movie deviant lurking about and chomping his teeth, waiting for the arrival of the 3:45 victim. Nature was predatory, man a killer, and I was prey to both. When I reached the end of the lane ten minutes later, after forcing myself not to run, I came out onto a street teeming with women shopping for groceries and instantly felt stupid, childish.

"Did you actually see a man in the woods?"

"Tell the doctor," my mother would say.

"Yes, he was nine feet tall and he looked crazy."

"Lying won't solve anything, son. I'm here to help you."

"He was there."

"Your son is obviously suffering paranoic delusions brought on by the disappearance of his father," the doctor tells my mother. "Give him one of those little green pills of yours whenever he seems tense. That should keep him in line."

As I walked down the crowded street I wondered if how I felt in the woods was what it was like for my mother. Terror and fleeting sensations of impending doom. I thought of her lying to my father's boss and then having to go lie down, feeling alone and ashamed and wanting to be in the dark. If my parents were here to protect Rudy and me, who was to protect them?

I stopped walking and checked my watch. It was only four o'clock. I didn't feel like going home yet. I looked down the street and saw a short line of people outside the movie theater. I started walking toward it and when I was a bit closer I saw that the picture had changed. "The Hustler" with Paul Newman was playing. There were mostly old men on line wearing caps and tattered jackets, looking around as if people were watching them, as if they felt they stood out because they had nothing better to do on a weekday afternoon, were alive but useless and alone. The box office was just opening and a woman wearing harlequin-style glasses was selling tickets. I got on line and waited. When I reached the booth I pushed a dollar through the aperture in the glass window.

"You can't go in," the lady said.

"Why not?"

"Children without guardians aren't allowed." She looked at me and the arched eyebrows above the cat-rimmed glasses indicated that I wasn't going to get my way. "No guardian, no ticket," she said.

"He's with me," a voice behind me said.

The ticket lady was as surprised as I was to hear this. I turned. Standing behind me was a man who looked to be in his early thirties. He had a mustache, small cynical eyes, and a cigarette dangling between his lips.

"He likes to pretend he's paying for himself. Gives him a sense of self-esteem," he said.

He looked down at me, his expression indicating that everything would be all right if I didn't say anything. He held his wallet open in his hands, thumbs hooked over each lip of it.

"Let me have two tickets," he said.

"He's not with you," the woman said. "He got on line by himself."

"I told him to meet me here. He's my nephew."

"What's his name?"

"MacDuff. What do you care? Just gimme two tickets."

"I can't let you in. I'm sorry."

The guy walked past me so that he could lean right up against the window. He was smiling as if he knew that the woman knew that the whole thing was secretly funny. He put his face close to the glass.

"I know you think you can't do it 'cause you'd be breaking the rules if you did, right? Well, let me tell you something, that's mind control. People are out there and their jobs, all they do all day long, is think up dumb rules to make you feel guilty with if you break them."

"I don't know what you're talking about."

"Come on. You let your friends slip in for free, right?"

"No, I don't."

"Well then this is your chance for excitement. If you let us in you'd really be going out on a limb. You'd be risking everything just so a poor little fat kid could see a movie."

What was this fat business, I wanted to know.

Then, suddenly, his tone changed, as if the game was over. "Look, what do you think we're gonna do, torch the joint? We wanna see a movie."

"I have people on line, sir."

"Yeah, and we're two of them. And the rest can wait until you give it up and sell us two tickets."

He was angrily pointing a finger at her while he spoke. His demeanor seemed to go through drastic changes, swinging from gentility to sarcasm to belligerence as automatically as the beating of a metronome. There seemed to be no stability to his moods, no subtlety or fine tuning, just rapid changes of personality. He seemed to be one large, exposed nerve, sensitive to the slightest stimuli. He stared at the woman in the booth. Clearly she would have to sell us tickets or call the manager. He wasn't going to give up. He slid a five-dollar bill through the opening in the glass. The woman in the booth let it sit there for a moment, then gave in and picked up the bill.

"Oh, what do I care for a dollar fifty an hour," she said, and she pushed forward two tickets and change.

"There. Was that so hard?" he said to her. He stuffed his money in his wallet, then turned to me. "Go ahead," he said, pointing to the theater door. He turned toward the street and, after taking one long drag on his cigarette, flicked the butt all the way to the gutter. I opened the door and he held it open above my head. I walked in, and he followed.

Once inside I was uncertain whether I was obligated to sit with him. I was a bit suspicious of his motives. I kept imagining his hand dropping onto my knee at some point during the movie. While Paul Newman was up there racking up thirty balls straight the sanctity of my privates would be invaded by a member of the Teamsters. The two of us walked through the huge lobby of the old movie palace, an art deco construction of the early thirties. He walked over to the candy and popcorn concession; I followed a few steps behind. He ordered a large popcorn and a Seven-Up, then turned to me and said, "You want anything?"

Not wanting to be indebted to a stranger who might demand repayment in the form of a sexual favor, I refused. "No," I said. "Thank you."

He paid the cashier. "I wanna go to the head," he said to me. This was it. My psychic sonar flashed red alert, anticipating the launching of his epidermal torpedo. But my paranoia was totally unfounded. He extended only the container of popcorn and the Seven-Up to me. "Hang on to these while I rinse a kidney," he said. "Go sit in the smoking section. I'll catch up with you." The guy was straight.

I went into the theater and found a seat. I stared at the gold brocades and sashes which held back the gigantic gold curtain framing the screen and nibbled at some popcorn. A few minutes later the guy joined me. He took off his worn leather jacket and laid it on the seat beside his. I was cradling the barrel of popcorn in my lap and he reached over and grabbed a fistful. He plucked each kernel from his right hand with the thumb and index finger of his left and popped them into his mouth one at a time. He sat silently, staring straight ahead at the screen. I wondered who he was. He had a small, curved scar the shape of a crescent moon at the top of one of his very high cheekbones. He could be anyone, I thought. He shoved the last few pieces of popcorn into his mouth with the palm of his hand, then brushed the salt off by smacking his mitts together like two cymbals. He reached over to his jacket pocket and removed a dull brass flask from the side pocket. The grandiose careers which I had begun to imagine for him were suddenly dismissed. It became apparent to me that it was more likely that he was replaying the events of a domestic squabble he had had with his wife as he stared at the screen, or else exorcising the dispiriting frustration and boredom he endured for a paycheck by fantasizing about punching out his boss. He unscrewed the cap and took a long slug from the flask. Then he set it down, letting it rest momentarily on his knee, before he brought it to his lips a second time and took two more swallows. He recapped the flask and slipped it back inside his jacket pocket. His bracer had relaxed him and he turned to me with a look of relief on his face.

"If I didn't drink, I'd have problems," he said. Then he laughed. "So why aren't you out playing with all the other little kiddies?" he asked me while reaching into the pocket of his shirt for the crumpled pack of cigarettes he carried there. He removed the pack from his pocket and jerked it upward, ejecting the unfiltered ends of three fags. He extended his hand in my direction and offered me a smoke.

"No, thanks," I said.

He shrugged as if to say that my refusal didn't matter to him. Then he pursued his line of inquiry. "So, like I said, why aren't you out in the sunshine?"

What was I supposed to do, tell him about my father? Tell him I couldn't stand being home?

"I don't want to be," I said.

He shrugged again, like, "Fair enough."

But then I unexpectedly said, "My old man split."

He sat there a moment, then raised his eyebrows, lowered them, and shrugged again. He waved my words away with the motion of one hand.

"No biggie," he said. "He'll be back."

He sounded sure of it. Then the lights were turned down and we sat and watched the movie in the dark.

After the movie ended we walked along Jamaica Avenue together, I going home because I had no place else to go, he going I didn't know where. He had really liked the movie; I wasn't too comfortable with it. On Paul Newman, up there on the screen in all those close-ups, losing looked romantic. But walking next to my unshaven friend who was drunk at six o'clock in the afternoon—thinking, too, about my father roaming the city with a busted nose, afraid perhaps to come home, and afraid not to—losing looked pathetic to me. This man and my father deluded themselves they were protesting the depravity of their lives. But they were no longer rebelling against anyone but themselves. No one cared what they did, outside of the small circle of their families, but they were unable to notice, too engrossed in fighting the phantoms of their own minds.

"Don't you have to go to work or something?" I said.

"Fuck it. I am at work."

"Yeah. What do you do?"

"I work for Ma Bell."

"Who?"

"The phone company, dunce."

At fourteen, I envisioned the telephone company as a highly efficient organization. I believed that it was made up of cheerful, fastidious technicians, an orderly and friendly place. Only my father was a misfit, an outcast, the aberrant cog in the smoothly running machine of nine to five. I looked at the half-drunk telephone worker. He was grubby and his clothes and gum-soled suede shoes were scuffed with dirt. He looked down at me, snickering.

"What are you looking at?"

"Nothing. I was just looking," I said. "Why aren't you doing any work?"

"Lunch time," he said.

"It's six o'clock."

"Coffee break. Look, kid, don't bust my balls, all right? I'm in the field seventy hours a week. I do enough. OK?"

We stopped at a corner and waited for a light. A gold Cadillac with two rich looking women in it drifted by us.

"Look at them. Bitches!" he yelled. "Yeah, everything's fucking wonderful, right? You bimbos!" They hadn't heard him. The light changed.

"I gotta go," I said.

"Yeah," he said. We stood there a moment. "Look," he said, "if it's a problem at home, don't sweat it. Split like your old man. He's got the idea. Take a break. Life is short, you know?"

I was fed up with him telling me what I should do. "My old man's got the right idea, all right! He's a fucking drunk. All the answers. Sure! Big man."

"Hey, fucko, I put in seventy hours a week. . . ."

"Yeah, you told me."

". . . To pay for a goddamn house I hardly ever see, days off that bimbo thinks I'd like nothing better than to build a fence or repaper a room. So don't give me any of that 'I only think of myself' horseshit. Let her go out and earn a buck."

"I don't want to talk about it," I said. I exhaled. "I gotta go."

"Yeah, well, fuck it. Go."

We were silent for a moment. He reached for his shades.

"I have to go," I said again. "Thanks for the movie."

He nodded. I turned and started walking. After a few moments, I heard his voice. "Run—while you can!" he shouted. Then I heard him laugh. But his heart didn't seem to be in it, and before I was out of earshot, he had stopped.

When I got home I caught some flak from my mother for staying out after school, but brushed it off; there was no spirit in her fight. My father, of course, had not yet come home, and there was no word when and if he would. I ate dinner by myself, then turned on the radio to catch the results of the day's game. While I was up, the telephone rang. I picked it up at the same time my mother answered on the extension in her bedroom.

"Hello."

"Lil? This is Charlie Pantano."

"Michael, if you're on, hang up. Charlie, I'm so sorry. I didn't have a chance to call."

"About what?"

There was a half-tick of hesitation before my mother said, her voice lightened by her surprise, "Your wife. I'm terribly sorry. Jack wouldn't let me go to the wake with him."

"What wake?"

There was a slightly longer pause this time. "Your wife's," my mother said. "That's why I sent the Mass card."

"My wife's sitting in the living room."

On that note of ludicrous shame, I hung up. There seemed to be an absurd quality overtaking the entirely pathetic side of the event. If nothing else, I had to admit that my father had a huge pair of balls. News came over the radio that Roger Maris had gone 0 for four that day; he had not broken Babe Ruth's record. This revelation did not disappoint me. Instead, it compounded the feeling that time had been split between acting and waiting—mostly waiting—and that just as the baseball world would not be complete that year until Roger Maris either hit or didn't hit his sixty-first home run, neither would my family's world be complete until my father returned, or we discovered for certain that he no longer would. I passed another day feeling helpless and frustrated. On Saturday, I decided to do something. I waited until my mother and grandmother left to pick up the dress my mother would wear to the wedding the following day, then went up to my room and began collecting Rudy and my grandfather.

CHAPTER SEVEN

My grandfather was wearing a suit, white shirt, and a tie when I discovered him sitting in the beaten-up old armchair in my bedroom. He was also wearing a fedora. When he saw me, he stood up.

"Shall we go?" he said.

"Go where?" I hadn't told him we were going anywhere yet and I wondered if he had some weird telepathic power, a perk of senility and near total obliviousness.

"To the wedding."

"That's not until tomorrow."

He looked down at himself. "Then why am I dressed like this?" he asked.

"How should I know?" I said, then walked to my savings bank to tally my funds.

"Are you sure it's not today?"

"Positive."

"Huh. I thought it was today."

"No such luck," I said.

Then he started to undress himself.

"What are you doing?"

"It's late. I'm going to bed."

"It's not late. It's nine A.M. Keep your clothes on."

"Are you sure?"

"Trust me."

He sat down again and brooded thoughtfully. "Is it possible that it's your birthday?" he said while I was counting my money.

"No, it's not possible. Why don't you just relax and just let it be Saturday, OK?"

I had nine dollars and eight cents altogether. Three upper deck seats to the Yankee game would cost four dollars and fifty cents, the subway ninety cents round trip. I had enough money to cover the ride and the tickets, but not quite enough for the indispensable extras—the yearbook, the program, the hot dogs and nuts. Perhaps even a cap. I looked at my grandfather. "Do you have any money?" I said.

"I don't know. Everyone says I lost it. I can't tell. It doesn't feel any different."

"Forget it," I said, and walked out of the room.

I went into my mother's bedroom and opened the second drawer of her dresser. Beneath several pair of stretch slacks and a few folded blouses was a small, beaded purse. It was where she kept all her savings. I unzipped it and took out a roll of bills. I knew that my mother had taken money for the dress with her that morning, and also some in order to have her hair done. I unrolled the notes and counted. There were seven one dollar bills. This was all the money we had left in the world. There was no bank account, savings, or stocks. How were we going to live, I wondered. During the course of my father's absence I had adjusted and functioned much as an amnesiac functions, I suppose. Each of us kept one foot in the real world, the world which goes to school, eats dinner, and watches television. We ignored what was happening as much as possible, just as I ignored my grandfather's senile and disconnected remarks. A part of each of us, I imagined, had given up on my father, secretly prepared itself for the news that he would not be returning. And that part of us had begun to live a new life, one separate from the inertia of our past, even if this new life seemed impossible and disorientingly unreal. Discovering that there was only seven dollars in my mother's nest egg, I began to wonder then just how we were going to accommodate the encroachment of reality upon the remains of our deluded and self-protective peace. I slipped the money back into the purse and left my parents' bedroom.

Downstairs, Rudy was lying on the living room floor. He was dressed in black shoes, black pants, and a green flannel shirt. He looked like a miniature Okie dirt farmer left over from the Depression. I knelt down on one knee beside him.

"Rudy," I said softly, "we're going to the Yankee game." He looked up at me. "It'll be outside, on the grass," I said. "It's nice to watch. I promise. And maybe Roger Maris will hit his sixty-first home run. What do you think? Sound good?" I waited for a sign to let me know he understood. Nothing. "We have to get out of the house for a little while, OK? Don't worry, it'll be good." He looked up at me a moment longer and then, almost instinctively—all hesitation vanishing—I reached out and stroked the back of his head. "OK?" I asked him. When Rudy looked at me again I felt as if there was nearly a sense of accord. "OK." I left him and went to make lunch to bring along to the game.

There wasn't much to choose from in the refrigerator. I made an egg salad sandwich, a peanut butter sandwich, and two bologna sandwiches, then wrapped them all in waxed paper and put them into a brown paper bag. When I went to replace the jar of mustard, three cans of beer standing on one of the shelves caught my attention. They were the colors of the flag and disquietingly familiar. They seemed to have acquired an iconic, almost hypnotic quality, like a magazine ad. I had seen them sitting on the lamp table in the living room beside my father's ashtray a thousand times, remembered their rank perfume from mornings when I was the first one up and had to take out the garbage. I had seen them held in my father's hand. I stared at them for several moments, then reached in and touched one of them with my hand. It was cold, smooth in an unnatural way, and reminded me of a bullet or a casket. Functional yet emblematic, it seemed laden with some absolving or unriddling key to identity—either my own or my father's, I did not know. I hesitated for a moment, then, sensing the release latent in it, stuffed the can into the bag along with the sandwiches, and grabbed the other two as well. I went into the living room, put Rudy's jacket on him, called my grandfather, and we left.

The three of us took the subway to Times Square, then changed to the Broadway local going uptown. The car was jammed with fans going to the ballpark, so I took both Rudy and my grandfather by the hand to keep them from getting lost. After a while, the train came up from the darkness of the tunnel and rose above the shops which lined upper Broadway. I stared out of the window, not talking to anyone. Occasionally, I looked down at Rudy. He was looking around as if he was seeing the world for the first time. I could not remember Rudy ever being on the subway before. He did not come to Radio City Music Hall for the Christmas and Easter shows with my parents and me; he was too young, they said. Rudy was peering around the waist of a burly man and staring out the window. The man, wearing grey chinos and a red flannel shirt, was hanging on to a balancing strap and reading a newspaper. He struck me as being either a truck driver or a mover. He was broad-shouldered and had forearms the size of bowling pins. He was wearing a blue Yankee's cap which was small for his huge head, giving him the appearance of being a child trapped inside the body of a brute. I turned back to Rudy, who seemed fascinated by the world passing by outside the train's window.

"Rudy," I said, "that's the Bronx." I gestured outside the window with a nod of my head. Rudy looked up at me but didn't indicate that he understood. "The Bronx is a borough of New York," I said. "It's part of the city, which is broken up into five parts. Why this is, I don't exactly know. It's your basic political thing, I think. Anyway, it's all the same city, only the Bronx is one specific part of it. If you have money, you live in Manhattan. If you don't, you live in the Bronx. Or Queens." Rudy stared at me mutely. "We live in Queens," I said. As I watched him, Rudy did something totally unprecedented. He nodded. As if he understood. I stared at him for a moment and he kept looking at me, as if he expected me to continue my history lesson. "You know what I mean?" I asked him. Rudy seemed to think this over for a moment, then nodded again. "You mean I'm not talking to myself when I'm talking to you?" Rudy seemed to be actually embarrassed by the question. Rudy seemed embarrassed. The thought itself was astounding. He looked at the floor of the subway car and shook his head. I laughed a single soft laugh in amazement, then put my hand on his shoulder. He remained still for a moment, steadying himself by holding on to the floor-to-ceiling pole between us. Then he let go, came forward a step, put his arm around my waist, and leaned on me. He kept his eyes on the floor for a moment, then turned his head sideways, resting it on my stomach, and looked up past the gargantuan man-child standing between himself and the window. A moment later I felt him relax and I knew that there was no need to ask him any more questions. I simply stroked his head as he clung to me, and with him looked out at the floating world I had told him was called the Bronx.

The three of us got off the train at 161st Street, along with hundreds of other fans. We walked to a ticket booth, waited on line, then bought a trio of seats in the upper deck. The noise of the crowd echoed through the concrete corridors as we hiked up the ramps to the top level of the stadium. The voices of the concessionaires selling programs and yearbooks filled me with a soft excitement, and I squeezed Rudy's hand. Feeling lighter already, I bought a program before we went up to our seats. While I was waiting for change, I eyed the Yankee pennant and the insignia caps. Rudy was standing next to me and I noticed him looking at the caps as well. "Come on," I said, knowing that I did not have enough money for two of them. "Let's go find our seats."

We sat near the top of the upper deck. The sun was shining and the grass was brilliantly green and fresh-looking. Though we sat in the sun, the air was cool and felt good. The expanse of the stadium and the bright, bleeding colors of fans seated across the stadium from us in the shade relieved me of the claustrophobic feeling I had had before coming out to the park. The sensation had begun two days earlier and had grown more acute in that time. All the commonplace occurrences of my days had suddenly become uncommon, each considered in the light of the fact that my father was gone. Everything I did or thought was effected by his absence, the result being emotionally like that of a funnel—everything was forced through the narrow aperture of his disappearance. I had begun to feel squeezed, then strangled, and finally suffocated. Now though, looking out at the crowd and the grass, the players taking swings in batting practice, the vendors in their red-striped shirts walking briskly through the aisles with their baskets held high above their heads, I felt myself swelling, filling up again with peace, like someone taking a deep breath of fresh air after years of being entombed. I saw how easy it was to forget what there was to love about the world, how easy it is to pity yourself.

Some of the players were running in the outfield, others were talking as they stood along the baselines. Rudy was watching the players taking turns in the batter's cage. Elston Howard lofted two balls in a row to deep center field. He had swung through the pitches, not overextending his swing, and the balls just sailed silently and slow, like birds gliding in the wind. The centerfielder caught them mutely, then lobbed the balls back to the infield. As I watched the warm-ups, I remembered the beer.

I had never taken more than one sip of beer at a time, either stealing some or asking for a taste from my father's glass out of curiosity, or a need for attention, the act confirming me, in a minor way, as an adult. Now that the drinking was my responsibility and not my father's, each breath seemed to catch in my throat before it was released. The paper bag sat between my feet. Leaving it on the ground, I reached down and unrolled it, then reached inside and felt beneath the sandwiches for one of the cans. Without bringing it above my seat, I popped the top with a metal opener, then slowly poured half of the beer into one of the paper cups I had brought along. I set the can down beside my foot and slowly sat upright. I checked to see if anyone nearby was watching me, or if any of them cared. No one seemed to. I looked down into the cup; in it was a cone of white, pockmarked foam. I put the edge to my lips and drank, the foam rising into my nostrils before the slow, sweet, syrupy musk of the beer touched my tongue. I had taken barely a sip. I sat there for a moment, exhaled, then put the cup to my lips again and swallowed deeply three times, wiped my mouth, and relaxed.

The beer seemed to caress my brain like a cool hand, and after a few minutes I felt dreamy. I turned my head and looked past Rudy at my grandfather. He was sitting with his legs crossed, one knee over the other, his hands in his lap. As he looked around, he seemed oblivious, as usual. A lot of people around him were wearing caps, but my grandfather was the only fan I could see who was wearing a fedora. Short, his upper body erect, he looked like an ambassador from some small, Mediterranean nation.

"Are you all right?" I asked him, leaning in front of Rudy. I waited for an answer, but my grandfather did not turn and face me. "Hey," I said, "are you in there?"

My grandfather finally turned and seemed puzzled to see me staring at him. "Yes?" he said, more in the form of a question than a reply.

"Are you comfortable?"

"Reasonably." Then, looking right at me, he said, "Where are we?"

"We're at Yankee stadium. A ball park."

"A ball park," he said. He seemed to mull this over for a moment, then said, "In that case, how about some peanuts?"

"Are you hungry? I have some sandwiches."

"No, I'm not particularly hungry."

"Then why do you want peanuts?"

He seemed to think about this for a moment. "I guess it's the ritual of it that appeals to me."

"Eating peanuts is a ritual?" I said.

"Aren't you supposed to eat peanuts at a ball park?" he said.

"Look, you can eat whatever you want."

"Well, I think the occasion calls for peanuts."

"Fine," I said. I looked around for a vendor, but didn't see any nearby. "There are no vendors around now," I said. "Wait a few minutes, and when one comes I'll buy you a bag."

"I have my own money," he said.

"Where did you get money?"

He shrugged, not in order to be mysterious, but as if he truly didn't know or care. He looked away, his head tilting back, his eyes staring aimlessly at the sky. I sensed that his fit of lucidity had passed and decided not to press his coherence, or near-coherence, any further. Still holding the cup of beer in my hand, I took another sip. The head had nearly dissolved and the cool, thick malt taste came through purely this time. It wasn't good, and it wasn't bad. I took another, longer sip. The easing of my feeling of claustrophobia was now beginning to give way to a slight feeling of euphoria, a sense of release. By the time I drained the cup my taste buds were numb and a lightness seemed to be singing in my limbs.

The ball park was filling up quickly now, the stands becoming crowded as swarms of people surrounded us, making me feel, perhaps for the first time in my life, singular and aware of myself, yet adequate and unashamed. The crowd was untainted and alive, a passive, essential mass. I refilled my cup then stared down at the crowd by home plate. People moving along the aisles to and from their seats were dabs of color and their movement was hypnotic. When I looked at the stadium clock I wondered where I had been for the past two minutes. They seemed to have passed like centuries. My arms began to feel rubbery and the afternoon and I seemed to be breathing each other in and out. It felt as if the space around me had become elastic and that it and I fit into each other, that it had become a glove cinched down snugly around me, and, feeling this, I laughed to myself. Without falling out of the dream, I watched as my grandfather waved to a peanut vendor. He did not manage to catch the man's attention. As I watched him, the almost fluid, in-and-out relationship he had with clock time and logic became clear to me, clear as the rigidity with which I had tried to define him lost its own firmness. Though he remained motionless in his seat, he seemed to change right in front of my eyes, his past, which lived in him, revealed for me to see. I saw him as a young man with dark brown hair combed straight back and parted severely in the style of the 1920s. Then I saw how he looked when I was a child. He had a more youthful face, leaner and sterner, as if the soul behind it held it together by an act of will. He was softer now, his features sinking into his flesh, and this softness seemed to open out around him like a parachute, slowing his fall, slowing it so that he seemed to float rather than plummet, as he descended toward the last days of his life. If he had seemed merely senile to me before, I now sensed that he was free. He required, less than any of the rest of us, the illusions of logic and causality, the rigors of identity and self. He could slip in and out of the world, whereas we could not. What to him was a dream was to us a trap. And no amount of struggling, it seemed, was capable of freeing us from it.

Batting practice was nearly over and Roger Maris was the last player to take his swings. I suddenly became interested in the measured world again. I watched him intently as he stood at the plate. He hit a few ground balls and then began getting his swing under the ball, driving pitch after pitch into the air. I began to grow excited, the hair on my arms stiffening as if an electric wand had passed over them. After watching him get into a groove at the plate, I glanced at Rudy and noticed that he was watching intently too.

"That's Roger Maris," I said to him. "Do you know who Roger Maris is?" Rudy shook his head. Then he took a chance. He pointed at home plate. I knew that he was guessing. "Yeah, that's him," I said gently, wanting to hold onto the thread which now seemed to be pulling us together. "Do you know what he might do today? Who he might become if he does it?" Rudy pointed to Roger Maris again. The literal nature of his response prompted me to think that his two or three direct answers earlier in the day had been flukes. "Rudy, do you understand what I'm asking you?" He nodded. "You do?" He hesitated a moment, then nodded again.

I sat there for a moment, watching him. The small startled eyes, the woe already carved into his face, a face that was one moment as innocent as sleep, young as any child's, and, the next instant, as aged by care, it seemed, as my grandfather's. "Rudy," I said, "can you tell me why you don't talk?" His lips grew smaller as he pulled them more tightly together, his breathing coming erratically now, in deep bursts like a bellows. He looked away from me and down at the ground between his feet. He couldn't say.

When Rudy was younger my parents had taken him to different doctors hoping to find out why he hadn't begun to speak. The tests they performed indicated that he could, if he wanted to. Why he chose not to was a problem which was referred to specialists who asked questions, rather than probed with tongue depressors and X-ray machines. Rudy was asked to draw pictures of what he saw in his head, then the results were examined. One of the specialists recommended that we leave Rudy alone, allow him to go about silently, and undisturbed. We were to let him draw pictures, if that was what he wanted to do, and come out of his shell on his own. The last specialist hypnotized him, and in his trance Rudy supposedly spoke. The doctor would not reveal what he said, only informing my parents that Rudy was deeply troubled, and that they should consider seeing a counselor themselves. After that, there were a number of late night arguments in my parents' bedroom, and Rudy was taken to no other doctors. We let go of him in some way then, allowed him to hover silently about the fringe of our lives, our dumb acknowledgement of his presence not actually an acceptance of him, or a rejection either, but undeniably a failure of responsibility. For my part, I ignored him as if he were a thing, some mutant, not my brother. My parents looked for other answers, ones which would not implicate them the way the findings of the specialists had.

I put my arm around Rudy and we sat there for a few moments, silently, as he would have it. Then Rudy reached over and put his hand on my leg and left it there. He felt safe, it seemed. Finally he felt safe, and that was enough. After another few moments had passed, I patted him on the back and said, "Come on, sit up. Watch Roger Maris."

I told Rudy that Roger Maris could become the first man in baseball ever to hit sixty-one home runs in a single season, and that he was only one short of breaking Babe Ruth's record. The next home run he hit would do it. And then Maris hit one out. Fans cheered, and Rudy pointed to home plate. He was excited, actually showing some emotion, and I hated to disappoint him.

"No, that's not a home run," I said. "At least not technically. It would have been a home run if he'd hit it during the game, but this is just, you know, practice. They have to be playing for real, and keeping records for it to count." Rudy stared at me blankly. "Do you follow me? It's like, for things to have meaning, there has to be a relationship with the past. Like, OK—we're brothers because we have the same parents. And mom and dad had parents, and that's a family. You see? The past. Relationship. Lineage." I was using my hands a lot, which meant I didn't know what I was saying. "OK, our lives have meaning in relation to mom and dad's life . . . or lives . . . sort of." Did they? How did my life and Rudy's intersect with our parents'? How deeply did the past inform the present? No matter what happened, I felt that Rudy was now my responsibility. So was that it? All is ephemeral unless we take responsibility for it? I took a sip of beer, then opened a fresh can. And as I got drunker, I wondered if my father drank because he could not, or would not, take responsibility for anything in his life, including himself. At that moment, my connection to Rudy, my obligation to him—my powerlessness in a sense—seemed to me even more acute, more mortally weighted. Accepting the responsibility of caring for him was freeing, but at the same time daunting, almost suffocating. I literally felt as if I were underwater. It was a paradox of freedom and arrest. Move your arms and you soared upward. The only trouble was, you couldn't breathe.

When the "Star Spangled Banner" began, I stood up with Rudy and everyone else. I felt wobbly, as if all the cartilage in my spine had turned to plant matter, a thin green stem which was barely able to support me. A voice from the row behind us began to growl a few bars into the anthem.

"Hey, Pop. Get up."

I looked over my shoulder and saw a man with a crew cut, the greenish-blue tattoo of a bulldog on one arm, and a face to match it. He was standing behind my grandfather, who had remained seated when the singing began. The man had a tremendous stomach covered by a shapeless, stretched-out T-shirt which was taut as a snare drum everywhere except for a half-dollar sized area over his navel. I didn't like the way he had spoken to my grandfather.

"Hey," I said, "what's your problem?" What's your problem? My father's expression. Beer in one hand, asking somebody, what's your problem. All I was missing was the Camel cigarette.

"It's the national anthem," the guy said. "Everybody stands."

People were beginning to look over at us now, the local, out-of-key singing giving way to the spectacle of public disagreement.

"He's old," I said. "He can sit if he wants to."

Someone turned and loudly said, "Shhh!"

I snapped my head quickly in the direction the voice had come from and thought, fuck you. And, like an after image, the doppelgänger of some harsh bright light, I saw in my mind's eye my father standing in the kitchen, my mother reproaching him, and his head snapping quickly to one side and his lips parting as he spit out the words, fuck you. Then the image faded from my mind like a movie scene being sucked into the void of a slow dissolve.

The guy behind me said, "I say he takes his hat off at least."

I stared at the huge, bitter figure standing above my

grandfather. Powerlessness. He must feel it all week long, all through his long shadow of a life. It's where the bitterness comes from. I reached over and gently lifted my grandfather's hat from his head. He never noticed. I looked at the man behind me. "OK?" I said. And, without another word passing between us, we came to a sense of agreement, and, perhaps, even achieved a minor measure of dignity for one another.

The Red Sox batted first, but didn't score. In the bottom half of the inning, the Yanks went down in order and Maris did not take a turn at the plate. Using a scorecard, I explained the game to Rudy. He seemed curious about the mathematical description of it, the abstract quality of meaning, the tiny checks and dashes which signified actions and constituted a language. The more beer I drank, the more loquacious I became. I began going off on tangents, digressing on subjects I wasn't even familiar with—at least, not until that moment. The beer lifted my spirits and everything seemed worth talking about, as if it all possessed something secret to be marvelled over, relished, and discussed. Baseball numbers. Letters, language. They were all living things, I said to Rudy. Not simply abstract, but alive. The only things which could ever truly be dead were the unimaginable. And the unimaginable didn't exist, right?

By this time I was on my third can of beer, had abandoned the cup, and was heavily into exploring the gonzo roots of metaphysics.

Maris flied out to deep center in the second. This seemed to bring me somewhat back to earth. Remembering that I had brought sandwiches along, I asked Rudy if he was hungry. He should eat something, I told him, and he reluctantly agreed to half a bologna sandwich in order to appease me. My grandfather was staring off over the long, curving sweep of fans to our left.

"What are you looking at?" I asked him.

Without looking at me he said, "I'm looking for a peanut vendor."

I'd forgotten about this. "OK, good," I said. "You're doing great."

He turned to me. "One question," he said.

"Shoot."

"What will he look like?"

I paused for a moment, holding the sandwich I was unwrapping for Rudy in my hand. "He'll probably be the guy carrying a basket full of peanuts," I said.

"No one in particular?"

"No. Just your basic peanut vendor. OK?"

As I handed Rudy his lunch, my grandfather's hand went up into the air. He had spotted one. The man saw him and began to climb the long, low steps two at a time. When he reached us he set his metal basket down on the asphalt step beside my grandfather. "How many?" he said.

"Well," my grandfather said, pausing as if the answer required scrutinous testing and consideration, "I think

I'd like one bag for myself. But there are my grandsons also, and they might like some."

"Don't give me your family tree. Just tell me how many you want."

"One more," I said, jumping in before the situation got ugly. Reaching into my pocket for change, I said, "That'll be two altogether."

"Congratulations, you can add." The vendor bent over and grabbed two bags with a vengeance. "Forty cents," he said.

When I looked up I saw that my grandfather had some oddly colored notes in his hand. They were blue and, for a moment, I thought they might be silver certificates, blue dollar bills I had seen once or twice. But the notes were too large to be dollar bills. He took one of them from the thin stack and unfolded it. It was the size of a sheet of looseleaf. Extending his hand, he held it out to the vendor, who was already making three other sales across the aisle. When he turned back to us he snatched the bill from my grandfather's hand, glanced at it quickly, then automatically began to stuff it into his apron. When what he was looking at registered, he said, "What the hell is this?"

"That's one share of Lupico stock," my grandfather said. "Extremely rare these days because they're out of business."

"What is this bullshit? I'm busy. Pay up."

"I have paid you," my grandfather said, trying now to open his bag of nuts.

"This is worthless, old man."

The man was looking down at my grandfather, scowling, impatient, full of an indiscriminate New York anger. "Here," I said. I handed him a dollar bill. He looked at me for a moment, grabbed the bill, made change, then tossed the stock certificate at my grandfather. It spun a few times in the air, then landed in my grandfather's lap, covering his hands and the bag of peanuts. "Go to hell," I told the guy, and he picked up his basket and bounded down the steps. Reaching across Rudy, I lifted the certificate from my grandfather's lap, looked at it for a moment, then handed it back to him. "I'm sorry," I said. My grandfather pursed his lips, then shrugged his shoulders, his jaws working on a pair of shelled nuts. In other words, there's no reason to regret what is impossible for you to prevent. Just endure it. I turned back to the field. Endure it, I thought. When I looked back at him a few moments later, he was sitting placidly, his legs crossed, shelling peanuts and nibbling on them like a squirrel. When he caught me staring he turned and said, "Now this is a ballgame."

Maris went hitless his next two times at bat. He came to the plate in the eighth inning for what seemed to be his last chance of the day. The crowd stood on its feet and cheered. I hoisted Rudy up onto my shoulders so that he could watch. "If he hits it out, that's it," I said. "It's over. Everything's changed." I thought about this for a moment and it struck me, in a way, as being terribly sad. Maris swung and missed, took a called strike, swung and missed again. The crowd's hope faded. People sat down, others began to leave.

We sat again. The sun had gone behind us and we were in the shade now. The autumn air was chilly and I noticed Rudy pulling his arms tightly against his sides. My grandfather had tucked one lapel of his jacket inside the other. I said I thought it was time we should go. I needed to use the men's room again and told Rudy and my grandfather to wait for me by the nearest concession. A few minutes later, I rejoined them. I took a Yankee cap from behind my back and put it on Rudy's head. "There," I said, "you're an official fan."

The three of us walked down the ramps with the other fans. The excitement was gone and I felt the weight of our disordered world returning. We climbed the stairs to the elevated train tracks, and waited.

From where we were standing I could see the sun setting to the southwest, over the Manhattan skyline. The sky was darkening, and the sun—distant, low, and cool—was a perfect circle. It seemed indifferent, unlike summer when it was fierce, or in bitter winter when it seemed to have forsaken us for our sins. The times when it had been judgemental seemed remote to me as I stood on the platform, looking out at it. I felt stark and alone, necessary in no fathomable way. I heard the rumbling of the train and when I turned to look for it saw Rudy standing beside me, staring up at me as if awaiting the return of my attention. I tugged the beak of his cap down over his eyes, and when he pushed it up he was smiling, unmistakably smiling. And then I felt good. And a moment later, deeply necessary.

Rudy and I stood by the front window of the first car, looking out at the tracks, my legs feeling stiff and heavy and weak. My grandfather was sitting and talking with a black man, who was seated beside him. The man wore sturdy, thick-soled black shoes which were highly polished, and carried a black lunch pail. When we changed trains I asked my grandfather what the two of them had been talking about.

"Dignity," he said, without looking at me. And before I could ask him what he meant, we were swept along by the crowd and on the opposite platform caught our next ride.

The train sped through the tunnels between stations, then slowed to a grind and came to a halt. Outside the windows, the walls of the tunnel were black. We sat quietly, my grandfather on one side of me, Rudy on the other. Everyone in the car was silent, either staring straight ahead at nothing, or else huddled inside the frail cave of a newspaper. My grandfather turned to me.

"I have something for you for your birthday," he said, reaching into his coat pocket.

"Gramps," I said softly, "it's not my birthday."

"It isn't?"

"No."

"Well, take it anyway."

"Why don't you just hold onto it till then?" I said. And then I realized that he would be dead soon. Somehow he knew it, and now he was telling me.

His hand emerged from his jacket holding a worn leather pouch. He opened it and took out sheets of paper which had been folded until they were the size of wallet photographs. As he began unravelling them, I saw that they were more stock certificates. Only some of them did not seem to be actually printed. As he shuffled through the small sheaf of paper, I saw that some of the certificates were completely illegible. They seemed to have been drawn by a whimsical hand. The details of the worthless but legitimate stocks had been replaced by a series of miniature tapestries. Brightly colored, playful and rudimentary as a child's free-hand drawing. Underwater creatures became geometric shapes with whiskers; the sun was a spider with an eyeball for a thorax. Tiny, flagellating, wide-eyed organisms—dollar signs in the shape of spermatozoa—bore the letters of the word Lupico heavenward.

"Here," he said, handing me the certificates.

I took them from him. "Are these really worthless?" I asked.

"Absolutely. You think I'd give you anything to worry about."

The train slowly began to move. "And don't lose the pouch," he said. "You're going to find you have a lot of crap to carry around. I hate to be so unsentimental, but that's the way it is." On that note, he closed his eyes and folded his arms across his chest. The train picked up speed until we were hurtling through the tunnel again. The lights in the car went out and the mechanical pandemonium of the train crushed my thoughts before I could turn them into words. I folded the certificates, put them inside the pouch, and slipped them into my pocket. I closed my eyes and, after several moments, the erratic rocking and clatter of the train began to feel like a clamorous peace.

CHAPTER EIGHT

When we got home my grandmother was standing in the porch, looking out of the window. She saw us coming down the street and I could see her worried look turn into a scowl. She began berating me the moment I stepped through the door. I walked past her without a word and when my mother saw me and realized that I was half-drunk, she raised her hand and tried to slap me. I caught her arm by the wrist.

"Let go of me," she said, trying to tear her hand free.

My grandfather was wandering directly toward the kitchen, free-floating through the house, not passing Go, not collecting two hundred dollars. My grandmother was unzipping Rudy's jacket, upbraiding me continually, sort of as background music, not even watching my mother and me. It was all so familiar and dispiriting that I gave in to it. My anger flew out of me in a single breath and I released my mother's wrist, remaining in front of her to let her know that I was willing to be struck if that was what she wanted.

"Where were you?" she said.

"The Yankee game."

"Who said you could go to a ballgame?"

"Who said you could get your hair done?" I said. The remark was so glib and disrespectful that it stunned her. She stood there as if I had shamed her into silence.

"Don't you dare speak to your mother like that," my grandmother said.

"Why not?" I looked at my mother. "You think you help us any more than he does?" I said, meaning my father. "You're never satisfied, he's never satisfied, and Rudy and I catch all the hell. You've had fifteen years to work it out. Finish it."

There was silence. A moment later my mother looked back at me and said, "Get out of my sight."

In my room, I took off my jacket and lay down on the bed. Within seconds I was pitched into a light sleep, my body seeming to rise and then plummet in space, and I dreamed. I dreamed of accidents. My father hitting the lamp-post with our car; falling off my bike and shattering my elbow when I was nine, my mother and father running down the street to help me in the otherwise tranquil summer dusk; a gash above Rudy's left eye, deep and glistening like the flesh of a cherry, the cut opened by something which had been thrown at him from across the room. Anger and accidents. Unintentional hurts and wounds we had bestowed upon one another in that house. Regrets over what we lacked the strength to prevent. I woke and bolted up in bed, my heart racing. Beside me the luminous hands of the clock glowed. I had drifted through dreams for two hours. I got out of bed and went to use the bathroom, then went downstairs to get something to drink. The television set was on. It was Saturday evening, eight-thirty—time for "Lawrence Welk." But my grandfather was dozing. I went over and gently shook his arm.

"Hey," I said to him, "'Lawrence Welk' is actually on. Wake up."

He opened his eyes, looked at me without recognition, then closed them again, and returned to his dreams. Rudy was curled up on the couch, his back turned to the room. I took an afghan from the back of the sofa and covered him with it, then went into the kitchen.

"Who said you could come downstairs?" my grandmother said.

I ignored her.

My mother was standing on a chair, wearing the dress she had bought for the wedding. My grandmother was on her knees hemming it. My mother didn't look down at me as she stood there, filing her nails.

"Get out of here," my grandmother said. "I don't want to see you."

I opened the refrigerator and took out a can of juice, filled a glass, then leaned against the sink while I drank from it. I looked at the low-cut back of my mother's dress. Dreamer, I thought to myself, still angry with her, unable, as yet, to move myself to sympathy, just as she would not be budged from her dreams.

"I'm not going tomorrow," I said.

"You'll do what you're told," my grandmother said.

"I'm not speaking to you," I said. I looked at my mother and said one more time, "I'm not going."

She ignored me, not saying a word. I held my glass up over the porcelain basin of the sink, then let it fall. Even as it shattered, my mother refused to look at me. But she understood, and I walked out of the kitchen, leaving behind my mother's self-protective and condescending silence, and my grandmother's desperate condemnations.

I was awakened by a pounding. I was on the couch and in the darkness I sat up. A white, ghost-like figure floated down on an angle some distance from me in the darkness, and then I heard footsteps and my mother's voice whispering to me. "Stay there," it said. There was more pounding and I realized that I had fallen asleep on the couch after taking Rudy to bed. I rose to follow my mother and saw the dim, cream-colord Nite-Lite go on in the kitchen. The pounding stopped for a moment and I heard my father's voice. It was shouting, "Open the goddamned door!" My mother was near the door when the pounding started again, alternating with my father's howling. She put her face near the small, hexagonal-shaped pane of glass as my grandmother came up behind me. "Don't let him in," she called to my mother. "I've called the police." I saw my father's face through the glass as the faint light sliced through the window. An X-shaped bandage was taped across the bridge of his nose and he was glaring through the glass at my mother. "Open the fucking door!" he hollered.

"Don't," my grandmother shouted.

My mother hesitated, then reached for the lock. My father's fist burst through the glass and my mother shrieked, falling to the floor, her hands clutching her face. My father's arm reached inside the door, searched for the lock, flipped it, and he stepped inside the house. He stood in the doorway, looking down at my mother, who was kneeling on the floor, crying. Then he looked up at my grandmother and me.

"I'm home," he said.

He was wearing what was left of his blue suit. The right shoulder was torn and the breast pocket was missing. In one hand he held a can of beer. Hanging by his side, it had the aura of a revolver.

"Get out," my grandmother said.

"Shut up."

There were footsteps moving quickly down the alleyway and up the back stoop. My father turned, made a fist, and cocked his arm to swing. The first policeman through the door caught his arm before he could, the second one came in and forced my father's arm behind his back. He dropped the beer can onto the linoleum tile and beer ran across the floor, pooling by my mother's knees. They forced my father up against the kitchen counter and, as he struggled, jerked him down onto the floor. One of them kneed him in the kidneys, the other pressed my father's face to the floor. "Don't move," the cop said. They had my father's arms behind his back and one of them reached around to the small of his waist and grabbed a pair of handcuffs from his belt. They forced my father's wrists together and cuffed him. He tried spreading his arms apart, but they were cinched tightly together. A moment later, he went limp. He gave in, or up, and his head dropped to the floor, and he was done.

One of the policemen stood up, looked at my grandmother and me, then went over to my mother and lightly touched her arm. "Are you all right?" he said. My mother, her face still pressed into her hands, shook her head. He stood up again. "Can you turn on some lights?" he said to my grandmother. He picked up the receiver of the wall phone and held it in his hand. "Why don't you go sit inside?" he said to me. Obeying his instructions instinctively, I turned and walked into the darkened living room. As I did, all I heard was the sound of the telephone's rotator wheel wind and unwind. Other than that, there wasn't a sound.

EPILOGUE

My father was put into my mother's custody, as she could press charges, and she had him committed to an asylum in Eastport, New York for psychiatric care. She visited him by herself every day, my grandmother refusing to go and, at first, forbidding Rudy and myself to go as well. Roger Maris hit his sixty-first home run, ending the season and the prolonged period of anticipation I had felt. I had expected that the new record would in some way change things, and, in one way, it did. Detractors claimed that Ruth's record was still the test, the standard, the constant in a world of flux. I had given up on the idea of constants, however. Everything was in a state of flux, I believed, of longing and motion, and the best I felt we could hope for in a world in which the illusion of order is untenable is someone who is willing to assume responsibility for us, and a capacity for forgiveness beyond our largest hopes.

After several weeks I was allowed to see my father. My mother had decided to let him come home. He had agreed to stop drinking, and his job would still be waiting for him. I was not allowed into the actual hospital, but my father would come to a window from which I would be able to see him. I sat in the lobby waiting for my mother as she visited with him, and when she returned she handed me a small brown paper bag.

"Your father bought you a present," she said.

In the bag was a small black flashlight. I took it out and held it, staring at it dumbly. As if she saw on my face the fact that I could not comprehend why I was being handed what I had been handed, could not fathom the unbearable helplessness that the gift represented, she said, "It was all he could buy for you here." We stood together silently for a moment, and then she said, "Please, don't blame us."

When I left my mother I walked across the parking lot and stopped on an expanse of dead grass from where I would be able to see my father. There were tall windows behind black iron bars spread out along the bottom floor of the building and, after a few minutes, my father appeared beside my mother in one of them. He was smoking a cigarette and wearing a sports shirt and a pair of chinos, his free hand stuffed into one pocket. We stared at each other across the distance and then my mother seemed to say something to him and he removed the hand from his pocket, held it up, and waved at me.

Please, don't blame us. I no longer had any desire for spite, or any defense against the truth. What I had come to know was that there was no place to lay blame, only a sadness which was beyond reproach. Slowly, I removed my own hand from my jacket pocket, held it up, and waved back.